A TIME TO KEEP SILENT

A TIME TO KEEP SILENT

Gloria Whelan

WILLIAM B. EERDMANS PUBLISHING COMPANY
GRAND RAPIDS, MICHIGAN

ISBN 0-8028-0118-8

For my daughter Jenny,
who believes in legends.

 ONE

I stopped talking so my father would listen to me. He spent his evenings sitting alone in his study with the lights out, like a blind person who no longer believed in the light. Even when he was with someone else he held his head a little to one side, as if he were listening to distant sounds instead of the voices of the people around him.

It was because my mother died. I don't let myself think about that. I won't ever go into a hospital again. When I visited her there, the world outside her window was like the picture on a postcard of a country you had never seen. But when I stood outside in the hospital parking lot looking up at her window, it was the room I had just left that seemed unreal.

At least my father talked to me then. And what he said made me feel better. That's his business. He's a minister. But after Mother died, he grew silent and preoccupied, seldom saying anything. He sat at the dinner table, his book open, reading to himself. That made me mad. Books ought to be for when other people aren't there. It was at dinner when it happened.

My father, myself, and our housekeeper, Mrs. Whittley, were having dinner, just sitting there moving food up to our mouths and chewing it, like those mechanical toys you wind up. I saw her look at my father out of the corner of her eye to see if he had noticed how she had gone to the trouble of making a rhubarb pie with a cinnamon-sugar topping. He hadn't. Mrs. Whittley was sociable and all that noisy silence bothered her nearly as much as it did me, so she started talking about some television program. She had a set in her room and watched it so much she called people like Oprah Winfrey and Rush Limbaugh and Arsenio Hall by their first names. She didn't have many friends besides us, and we weren't much use. "Arsenio had this man on last night who tried to teach him to take a drink of water standing on his head," she said. "Arsenio kept spilling it all over himself. You never saw anything funnier."

My father just went on reading. I would have said something, but it wasn't me she had baked the rhubarb pie for. She must have figured talking to me was better than nothing, though, because she turned and asked in that high, cheery voice people use when they talk to children, "Are you going out tonight, Clair? If not, you might like to see the special that's going to be on TV. All about the poisons they put in foods to make them taste better. I'm sure you'd find it educational."

I looked at my father. In better days he would have winked at me. His book with its scary title, *Fear and*

Trembling, was propped open in front of him. I decided not to answer Mrs. Whittley.

By now the poor woman was desperate for the sound of a human voice. "I asked if you were going out tonight, dear." There was a hint of impatience in her voice. You could see she thought she was working for a houseful of crazies.

My father raised his head, sort of swimming up, glassy-eyed, from the depths of his book. "Mrs. Whittley asked you a question, Clair." He was waiting for me to answer so he could go back to reading.

At first I had kept quiet because I wanted to, but suddenly I found I couldn't utter a simple "yes" or "no" to save my life. I could have screamed and shouted that I was miserable and that the whole world was upside down. But they didn't want to hear that, and nothing else would come out.

My father and Mrs. Whittley exchanged glances. "Clair, if this is your idea of a joke you're carrying it too far. You're being discourteous to Mrs. Whittley." My father was a very polite man, so "discourtesy" was about like murder would be to someone else.

I didn't want to hurt Mrs. Whittley's feelings. She had taken good care of us since my mother's death even if we were too quiet for her. I think she would have liked to be working for a family like Roseanne's on TV where a catastrophe was sure to happen every thirty minutes. Our catastrophe had already happened before she ever started working for us. I made an effort to open my mouth and get out a few words. My mouth opened all right, but nothing happened.

My father, who had been frowning while all this

9

was going on, now looked just plain scared. I was a little scared myself, although in the back of my head I guess I believed if I really wanted to I could start talking anytime I pleased. But later I discovered that even when I was alone I wasn't able to say a thing. It was as though I had forgotten how to talk.

For the first few days my father and Mrs. Whittley treated my silence as though it would go away if it were ignored. Like the advice newspaper columnists give you for handling kids who wet their beds or won't eat. When that didn't work, they changed their tactics and dragged me to our family doctor, who tried to have a confidential chat with me, but that's hard to do with someone who won't answer you.

At school my teachers fell all over themselves being "understanding" about my refusing to talk. You could tell how their minds worked: "Poor girl, she's all shaken up about losing her mother. We won't push her." They even seemed a little excited to have a kook in their class. Like I was good for a term paper in some night-school course they were taking on child kooks. They'd call on me and I wouldn't say anything. They'd smile knowingly and look a little sad. Then they'd call on someone else. But it finally got to them. By the end of April their eyes were beady and their mouths twitched when they had to deal with me. I overheard my math teacher call me "a stubborn mule." I didn't blame them. Everyone's allowed to be sick just so long; then it's a drag.

I went to an expensive private school that didn't cost my father anything because he was the school chaplain. The school paid their teachers a lot not to lose their tempers, so if you got in trouble you always went to a counselor before you went to see the principal. In May Mr. Dipple, the head counselor, called me into his office. He said he knew I must be unhappy about my mother's death, but couldn't I see that my behavior was disrupting classroom discipline?

I liked Mr. Dipple. He wore a T-shirt with Sigmund Freud's picture on it and drove a Vette and came to the noon dances and Texas two-stepped, not with the pretty girls, but with the dogs no one else would dance with. Only that after a while everyone caught on, and if he danced with you, you knew you were a dog. Still, he meant well.

When I didn't answer him, his voice grew reproachful and then wheedling. "Clair, you've always been a good student. You're a bright girl. You can see we can't have one set of rules for you and another for the rest of the students."

When I still didn't say anything, he let out a deep sigh that made Freud's beard quiver. Then he sent me back to class. I knew I was in trouble that noon when he walked over and asked me to do the lambada.

Things weren't improving at home. Mrs. Whittley spent more and more time in her room watching television, as if my silence might be catching. My Aunt Marcia and Uncle Keith, who lived nearby in a big house, started coming over a lot. My Uncle Keith was an orthodontist who fell all over himself to be pleasant to kids, making stupid jokes and then poking you in the belly to let you know he had come to the funny part. It drove him crazy that all the kids whose teeth he was wrenching into place probably hated his guts, so he set out to be jolly like a Santa Claus who smelled of mouthwash.

My Aunt Marcia was more quiet and settled. You can't have two clowns in a family, or nothing gets done. She was an interior decorator who had this habit of moving our furniture and rearranging our pictures every time she came to see us. My mom used to ask her please not to do it because we lived in a parsonage. That's what all ministers live in. The house and the oriental rugs and the green sateen drapes and the Chippendale-type couch covered in something that sounded like "cruel" and even the pictures that hung on the walls belonged to the Westville Heights United Church. The women on the house committee had put everything where they wanted it and they expected it to stay that way.

I knew I ought to be grateful for living in such a nice house. I had visited other ministers with my parents and seen how different from ours most of their homes were. But between the committee and Aunt Marcia I sometimes felt like I was living in a doll house and a big hand might come down and sweep everything away. That's what finally happened, but I didn't know it was going to be my father who would do it.

My father was getting more and more bothered by my refusal to talk. He no longer read at the dinner table. Finally I was more interesting than his old books. I'd catch him looking at me like a dog who has just been kicked by someone who had always been nice to him. I knew I had gone too far. I was just about ready to start talking when he scared me speechless all over again by announcing that he was going to give up his job as pastor of the Westville Heights United Church and start a mission in the northern part of the state.

I suppose a mission sounds like it has to be in a place

where it's hot all the time and your front yard is full of lions. That's not true. You can have a mission anyplace. As far as I knew, the only requirement was that you had to be uncomfortable most of the time and not too sure whether anyone wanted you.

For years I had heard my parents talking about going up north to live. They had spent their honeymoon there, and I guess they liked all the trees and the water and the little towns. They would bring it up whenever something irritating happened, like the time some of the congregation complained about my father's inviting poor kids from the city to our summer Bible school because they thought the kids might give us bugs. My mother would say to my father, "We should have gone up north when you wanted to, Dave." And he'd insist he never really wanted to. But anyone listening to him could tell he was just being polite.

Once I overheard my mother tell her sister — that's my Aunt Marcia — "If everyone in our family hadn't had a fit at the thought of me grubbing around in a small town, Dave would be doing what he really wanted to."

Aunt Marcia's answer to that was, "You should be grateful to us for helping David get the church in Westville Heights. He's one of the most successful ministers in this state."

My mother shot back, "What you don't understand is that Dave's idea of success and your idea are two different things."

Now my father was finally going off to the woods, and he was dragging me with him. Probably if I hadn't stopped talking it would never have happened. I had that awful kind of anger you get when something terrible happens to you and you know it's your own fault.

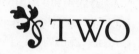 TWO

As soon as they heard the news, the church's board of trustees panicked. They sent for the president of the synod, Reverend Blakely, who spent a whole morning locked up in my father's study, with Mrs. Whittley carrying in about a hundred cups of coffee. When they finally came out, Reverend Blakely was saying, "David, I hate to see you turn yourself into a hermit. You have to live in the world to serve it. Did I ever tell you about the man I converted on the eighteenth hole of a golf course?" But he didn't change my father's mind. Neither did Uncle Keith and Aunt Marcia, who started treating my father like an invalid and me like a victim.

As for me, I moped around a lot, dragging my feet and flinging myself into chairs. It didn't help. The moodier I was, the more determined Father became. The day before we were to leave he called me into his study. When I was little he had let me sit there on Saturday afternoons while he wrote his sermons. I couldn't read then, but I liked to turn over the pages of his Greek and Hebrew books. The strange letters suggested secrets. When he was finished, I would ask him to give the sermon and he would solemnly thunder out one of the nonsense poems from *Alice in Wonderland*. "'Twas brillig, and the slithy toves" — he'd fling out an arm here — "Did gyre and gimble in the wabe; All mimsy were the borogoves, And the mome raths outgrabe."

On Sunday mornings when I heard the same voice and saw him use the same gestures, only this time with serious words, I would clutch my mother's hand to keep from giggling. This would make my mother want to giggle, and there we'd be, the minister's wife and daughter at the front of the church, struggling to keep from laughing at the sermon.

After church my father would frown darkly at us. "It did not escape my attention," he would say, "that during my exceptionally edifying homily this morning, there was an irreverent, no, a *disgraceful* lack of attention on the part of two parishioners who shall be nameless. However, they will not go unpunished and are hereby notified that as of four P.M. this afternoon they are to accompany me to the Westville Heights ice-cream parlor where they will be forced to sample all thirty-eight flavors, including the dreaded grape-malted-peanut-salted-cheese-chocolate-raspberry-ant crunch."

In the last couple of years the only time I had been called into the study was when I had done something wrong. Like accepting five dollars from Mr. Batten, who was running for the school-board election, to put his campaign literature in all the hymnbooks. So I was a little nervous when my father summoned me.

The study floor was covered with boxes of books.

15

The top of his desk, which was usually heaped with papers, didn't have a thing on it. He sort of smiled at me over the naked desk and said we would have a "person to person" talk.

"I just want you to know, Clair, why I've decided to leave Westville Heights and start a small mission up north." He looked at me with his head tilted down so he could see me with the top part of his bifocals. "When your mother was taken from us, I had the feeling that God was telling me I had been hanging on too hard to things: a comfortable home, a big parish and the salary that goes with it, a membership in the country club, a private school for you. That's a long way from the early Christians who owned nothing at all. When your mother died I decided the more tightly we hold on, the more we lose. I'm going to let go of everything and see what happens."

I guess he could tell by the way I sat slumped in the chair with my chin on my chest that I didn't agree with him because he said, "I know I'm not being entirely fair to you. You've grown up in Westville Heights. You've never known anything else. But your refusing to talk these last months has shown me more clearly than anything you might say that you aren't happy. As for myself, my congregation's growing too large. I'm marrying and burying people whose names I don't even know."

He could see he wasn't getting anyplace with me, so he ended up telling me to look on the whole thing as an "adventure." That was what he always said when he was desperate, so I knew my silence had gotten the better of him. I just sat there until he told me to go upstairs and finish my packing.

I didn't, though. I went for a walk. It was my last night in Westville Heights and I think I wanted to memorize as much of it as I could. It had been the same when I knew how sick my mother was. I kept looking at her so I would remember her face. But even in this short time it had become as indistinct and distant as the markings on the moon that was starting up the sky as I walked out of our house.

It was early June and the dogwood was in blossom. In the dim light its pink flowers hardly seemed to touch the black branches. The tops of the maple trees floated like dark clouds around the large houses on our street. I knew the names of almost everyone who lived near us, but unless they had kids my age I didn't really know them. They all had automatic garage-door openers so that you never saw anyone walk out of their house. The garage door would go up and a car would shoot in or out and that was it. The only time you actually saw people was if you got up early when the joggers were out, running all over like a disturbed ant nest, but they passed you by without saying a word. You might as well have been a tree or a lamppost.

An old car pocked with rust spots and with a fender missing drove slowly down our street. Several young children were hanging out of the windows staring at the houses. On summer nights cars like that often drove across the city limits into Westville Heights, where it was cool and green. They made me think of myself coming back one day, looking at everything that was so familiar to me now with the eyes of a stranger.

When I got back to our house my father's study door was shut and Mrs. Whittley was in her room

17

watching TV. No one heard me go up the stairway to my bedroom. On my yellow shag rug was a box I had packed with my stereo and my peanut-butter machine. There was a French cookbook, too. My father said I'd better be prepared to do the cooking and I knew I'd need some help. Mother was a fancy cook and liked to do things herself, so I never had much practice. I could have taken a cooking class at school but I chose manual training so I could make my father some bookends for Christmas.

A suitcase was lying open on my bed. My father had told me to take only what I "needed" because our house up north would be small. But how was I to know what I was going to need? There were Westville Heights families who went north each summer to a resort on Lake Michigan called Blue Harbor where they played tennis and swam and sailed. I had packed my tennis whites and a bathing suit and my Topsiders and a new dress that was sort of old-fashioned with a long calico skirt. I guess I thought I would play tennis in the morning and homestead in the afternoon.

I held the dress up to me and looked in the mirror. People never told me I was pretty. Instead they'd say, "one day" or "when you're older" you'll be very attractive, Clair. A lot of good that did me now. I was tall for thirteen, taller than most of the boys in my class, and skinny with kinky red hair that wouldn't straighten. My eyes were green with flecks of brown "like speckled birds' eggs," my father said. I had pale white skin like my mother's. "Clair of the moon," she used to call me.

Thinking of my mother made me more miserable than ever. I wondered if, when I left the house next day, the memories of her would come with me or if they would stay in the house like all the furniture and pictures and belong to the new minister's family.

❧ THREE

There was a moment the next morning when I thought my father was going to change his mind about leaving Westville Heights. He stood in the driveway, a suitcase in either hand, staring up at the house. To no one in particular he mumbled, "Am I leaving this place or going to another?" Weird statements like that came from reading his *Fear and Trembling* books. Then he swung his suitcases into the back of the new station wagon.

The station wagon was the only thing that morning that kept me from falling apart. It was a farewell gift from the congregation. One of the vestrymen, Mr. Olsen, was a car dealer. He had brought the station wagon over earlier in the week and handed my father the keys. "We thought this might be useful up north, Dave. You can fill it up with firewood or a bear carcass, or whatever else you'll be toting around up there in the wilds."

My father had started to say he couldn't accept a gift like that, but Mr. Olsen had cut him off. "You can't hurt the congregation's feelings, Dave. You've been here twelve years and we owe you a lot. We'll never find someone who suits us as well. Just don't forget we're not making any decisions on a permanent pastor until we hear you're sure you've made the right move. Personally, I'll never forget how you helped Evelyn and me through that rough spot — "

Mr. Olsen stopped himself, remembering I was there. He turned to me. "Don't you let your dad get rid of this car, honey. I loaded it with everything I had." He showed off the automatic window openers and door locks and the radio with four speakers, the mirrors that worked from the inside, and the seats you could raise and lower and tilt. He had a diamond ring on his little finger, and as he moved his hand around demonstrating how everything worked, the diamond shone in the sun like one of those flashlight pointers lecturers use when they show slides.

The more things Mr. Olsen demonstrated, the more disturbed Father became, but Mr. Olsen was like a kid with a new toy, so there was nothing much my father could say until he was gone. Then Father groaned, "How in heaven's name can I start out trying to live a simple life with a car like this?" Personally, I had fallen in love with the bright blue wagon the minute I saw it. When I heard my father complain, I was more sure than ever that there was something wrong with his mind.

As we drove away from the only house I had ever lived in, I made myself stare straight ahead by telling myself I was Lot's wife and would turn into a pillar of salt if I looked over my shoulder. My father didn't look back either.

Once we got on the crowded expressway, though, I

began to feel better. There was something about seeing all those people on their way to work that made our trip seem like a vacation. Then I remembered that we wouldn't be coming back and I felt miserable again.

I had to admit that the last few months had been rough. Since I had stopped talking I had lost a lot of friends. Some of the kids had even started to harass me, doing things like cutting in ahead of me in the lunch line to see if I would say something. Or sneaking up behind me and shouting to try to make me cry out. I suppose it was my own fault. They must all have thought I was a little crazy. I wondered if I would be able to make friends up north without talking. Even if I didn't I decided I wouldn't say a word. If my father thought dragging me away from Westville Heights would cure me, I'd show him how wrong he was.

I turned on the radio and got a rock station, adjusting the stereo so I was covered by the music. I glanced at my father. Ordinarily he complained about rock. "Why are those young men screaming so? They must have broken their legs from hopping about. Or perhaps their heads hurt? Perhaps some charitable person has hit them all soundly over the head with their own record albums." But that morning all he said was, "*Four* speakers. I'll never forgive Olsen." I think he was glad to have something to fill the hole my silence made.

He drove holding onto the steering wheel like it was a life preserver. He wouldn't even stop for lunch. Mrs. Whittley had packed sandwiches and we ate as we drove along, olives rolling onto the floor, salt spilling on the front seat, juice from tomatoes dribbling onto our clothes.

It was afternoon by the time we swung off the expressway and pulled up at a supermarket. My father took a ten-dollar bill out of his wallet and gave it to me. "Better get something for dinner and breakfast."

I was pleased and worried at the same time, glad my father trusted me to do the shopping but worried about what to buy. I had often ridden my bike to the Westville Heights Farmers' Market, which wasn't a farmers' market at all but a place where you could find things like strawberries in January and smelly cheese and cookies in tins with French words written on them. They even had little stools where you could sit down while they filled your order. I was told what to buy when I went there and I never saw the prices. They went on our charge. We had a charge everywhere. My father used to say if he ever dropped his wallet he could play fifty-two pickup with his credit cards.

Inside the supermarket women were pushing carts around with the same dazed expression on their faces I had seen that morning on the faces of the drivers who were going to work. It looked like they were getting messages from outer space about what to buy. But I was on my own.

I decided on steaks and chose two large ones. I thought Father could barbecue them. That way he wouldn't find out right away how little I knew about cooking. I wheeled the cart to the dairy department and feeling rather proud of myself remembered to pick up butter and milk. I got some raisin bread and peanut butter and had the man at the produce department weigh up a big bunch of grapes to munch on in the car. The man put a price sticker on the plastic bag and handed it to me. I glanced down and saw

$3.23! I thought it must be a mistake. I looked at the price on one of the steaks — $6.82! My face was burning. I put the steaks back and dropped the grapes on a shelf when no one was looking. Then I reached for a package of hot dogs and headed for the check-out counter. The total was four cents less than $10.00.

When I got back to the car, Father was studying a map. "Still a way to go," he said, rubbing his eyes and stretching. "I feel like I've been in this car for a week." He swung back onto the road. We found ourselves driving beside a lake so wide you couldn't see the other side. Along the beach were large summer homes like great wooden ships tied to the shore. We passed resort towns with candy-colored stores that sold antiques and sports equipment and neat clothes. It wasn't too different from Westville Heights. I began to feel better.

Then the lake vanished and we were driving up and down hills. At the bottom of the hills were farms with ramshackle barns and rows of tall pines on their western boundaries. "They're planted there to keep down the winter winds," my father said. That didn't sound too encouraging.

The towns grew smaller and older. Instead of gift shops there were hardware stores and something called feed stores and dark, dingy-looking bars with red neon signs and trucks parked outside. I began to worry again.

We were passing through a particularly tacky town that wasn't much more than a couple of battered store-fronts when my father slowed down. "I suppose I should have realized the larger, more attractive villages would all have churches by now," he said. He sounded disappointed.

With a sinking feeling I realized I was looking at the town where my father would have his mission. I studied the meager cluster of small wooden houses, wondering which one ours would be. But we turned away from the town and onto a sandy road that led toward the green wall of woods on the town's edge. Clouds of dust rose up around the car, floating in through the windows and powdering our clothes. Along the sides of the road a layer of fine dust had settled on the trees and bushes, turning the green foliage a dirty gray. Once we frightened two large black birds sitting in the middle of the road feeding on something dead. As the car came close, they flew off barking like dogs.

It was nearly dark when we pulled up in front of a little stone house that stood by itself on the deserted road. It was about the size of our garage in Westville Heights. The roof of the porch which ran the length of the house was supported by four rotting posts. The windows were shuttered and the yard was a snarl of overgrown grass and weeds. I looked at my father, hoping there was some mistake. His face was set, as though he were about to take an evil-tasting medicine that he knew would be good for him but which he first would have to get down. "It's a little farther from the town than I had thought," he said. "I suppose that's my fault. I told the real estate people it might be pleasant to have a little countryside around us."

Countryside, I decided in disgust, was what was left after you took all the good things away.

 FOUR

I followed my father out of the car, wondering what kinds of things might be hiding in the tall grass. At the entrance to the house there was a little battle between my father and the front door, which seemed to be stuck. Father gave it a kick. That surprised me. He wasn't a man to kick doors open. He liked to take his time and figure things out.

Inside, the house was dark. When Father reached for the light switch, nothing happened. "Real estate agent must have forgotten to have the lights turned on," he said, uncertainty creeping into his voice. The uncertainty made me feel worse than ever. If *he* didn't know what he was doing, what was going to happen to me?

He went out to the car to get a flashlight, leaving me standing there alone in the dark room. When I heard something rustling around the floor I decided to wait on the front porch. It was strangely quiet outside. There was no hum of lawn mowers or the splat of a tennis ball

26

being swatted back and forth. You couldn't hear cars driving by or children calling to one another. There was only the wind rubbing the tops of the trees in the woods behind the house.

When my father came back with a flashlight and shone it around the dark interior we could see a tiny kitchen, a living room, and a couple of bedrooms about the size of clothes closets. In the middle of the living room there was a table covered with a square of worn plastic. Around the table were four wooden chairs. Two more chairs stood against the wall. Against the opposite wall was a davenport covered with fuzzy green material that made it look like a large caterpillar. Old newspapers and dried leaves were on the floor. I thought of what my Aunt Marcia or the house committee of the Westville Heights church would have said.

Father dropped the grocery bag on the table, and I knew we were going to stay. "How about a glass of water?" he asked me. He turned the faucet on in the kitchen sink, but no water came out. "I should have known the pump wouldn't work without electricity." He led me out into the yard, where he began to work an old hand pump. After some strangling sounds there was a gush of water. He smiled. "At least something works. Taste it," he coaxed.

I cupped my hands to catch the water and drank some. It was icy cold and delicious. I had never thought about the way water tasted before.

"We'll do our unpacking tomorrow," Father said when we were back in the house. "Tonight we'll make up the beds and put together a little supper." He peered into the grocery bag.

I was afraid he was going to be disappointed, but if he was he didn't show it. "Hot dogs. *Chauds chiens. Perros calientes. Heis Hunds.* An international favorite. Excellent choice."

I was relieved that he wasn't critical about my shopping, but it upset me to see him so cheerful all of a sudden. The truth was I didn't want him to be happy. I didn't want him to like it there.

"I'll just build a little fire in the fireplace and we'll get some sticks to grill the frankfurters . . ." He looked sheepish. "I don't have any matches."

I had matches in my purse but I didn't want to let my father know. I always carried them to pretend to my friends that I smoked. I hated having them consider me out of it because I was a minister's daughter. If I gave him the matches he would know why I had them and he was always warning me about smoking. Still, I was starved and all I could think about was hot dogs sizzling over a fire. I took the matches out of my purse and handed them to him.

He gave me a long look. "For candlelight lunches in the school cafeteria?" he asked. In spite of the teasing tone his eyes were serious. But that was all he said.

When we went outside to gather dried tree branches for the fire, he looked at the rotting porch posts and front steps and mumbled, "Hard to tell where the kindling stops and the house begins."

There was a small hut in the backyard. I pointed to it and raised my eyebrows inquiringly.

"I'd forgotten how limited your experience is," he told me. "Didn't see any bathroom in the house, did you?"

28

I was stunned. I mean how primitive can you get?

"It's true it's outside, Clair, but at least it's inside outside."

I went stamping back into the house. Let him struggle around in the dark picking up old sticks. "Try to think of it as an adventure," he had said. An adventure was supposed to have some good things in it. Where were the good things in this miserable shack?

A minute later Father followed me in and laid an armful of wood next to the fireplace. "I thought it smelled fishy in here," he said. He was holding up the skeleton of a fish. "Someone must have broken in and grilled themselves a fish dinner." He built what looked like a teepee in the fireplace with some sticks. "Didn't know your father used to be a boy scout, did you?" He was ignoring my temper tantrum, but I didn't want it ignored. If I had been talking I would have told him exactly what I thought of his grotesque countryside.

The dry wood caught fire. As the heat started to rise in the chimney there was a loud scrabbling sound on the roof. We ran outside just in time to see a raccoon shinny down a drainpipe and scurry off toward the woods. It climbed the first tree it came to, rolled itself into a ball, and stared accusingly down at us, black eyes shining out of a black mask.

Father laughed, but I wasn't all that happy about sharing a house with a strange animal. "So that's where the fish came from," he said. "The raccoon must have mistaken the chimney for a tree hole. Looks like *we're* the trespassers."

We sat in front of the fireplace eating our hot dogs. Father had said grace, but it was a weird one: "Lord,

29

make room in the woods for two more of your creatures and let them learn from the wildings to take no more than their share." When dinner was over he spent a lot of time poking around at the fire, his back turned to me. Finally he said, "Clair, I know you haven't been very happy with me for taking you away from Westville Heights and bringing you to a place like this. I want you to know that if at the end of six months you want to go back, I promise I'll take you."

That meant we could be back in time for Christmas. My father turned around just in time to see my fingers moving as I ticked off the months.

That night I lay in bed, surrounded by unfamiliar shapes. I had never realized how much a part of my life inanimate objects had been. In Westville Heights my fourposter bed, my dresser, and my desk had been old friends standing guard over me at night. Now, the strange dark shapes around me seemed ominous.

Something ricocheted against my window screen. In the moonlight I could see a large beetley-looking bug. There were holes in the screen. What if the bug got in? I considered getting up and closing my window, but I didn't much like the thought of walking across the floor in my bare feet. Suppose I stepped on something soft, or worse, something that moved under my foot? I huddled into a ball like the raccoon in the tree had and thought about writing my Aunt Marcia and Uncle Keith. If they learned how unhappy I was, maybe they would come and take me back to Westville Heights.

Something brushed by my head. Startled, I sat up and looked around. Black wings were swooping toward me. Yanking at the sheet, I threw it over my head and ran out of my bedroom and through the front door. I raced for the station wagon, flung open the door, closed it quickly after me, and scrunched down in the back seat with the sheet over my head. The station wagon, I decided, was the only safe place to spend the night. It was comforting to think that some of the air inside it might still be from Westville Heights.

I had been too ready to go along with my father's lunatic ideas just because I felt sorry for him. What about my own feelings? What would my mother say if she could see me cowering in the back of a station wagon in the middle of the night? I wished I had my matches. I would burn the stupid house down. Only stones didn't burn. When I couldn't get any angrier, I began to feel better. I unwound myself from the sheet and looked out.

In the moonlight the stones of the cottage appeared to be white and the dusty foliage frosted with silver. I looked up at the moon. The pale face that looked down at me could have been my own — or my mother's. You weren't supposed to pray to people — only to God — but I looked up hopefully.

 FIVE

The sun shining in through the windshield woke me up. I hurried into the cottage, anxious to get into my room before my father saw me. But he was already up and dressed. The shutters were off the windows and wide yellow ribbons of sun lay over the furniture and floor. There was a fire in the fireplace, and the house seemed less damp and cold.

"I thought the raccoon had come back for you until I saw the corner of a sheet hanging out of the station wagon." Father was smiling, but his eyes looked worried. "What happened?"

I took him into my bedroom and pointed out the hole in the screen, ashamed now at my hiding in the car.

"Bugs?" he asked. I shook my head and waited for him to ask me more questions, but he only said, "Get yourself dressed and we'll have breakfast. Then I'm going into town to see about having the electricity turned on. You can begin to clear up some of the litter in here."

32

I didn't want to stay in the house alone, but his voice was firm. He was angry because I wouldn't talk and tell him what had frightened me. Most of the time he tried to ignore my silence, but I knew it upset him. I think he had hoped if he could just get me off someplace new my problems would stay in Westville Heights. But even I knew better.

After I watched the blue station wagon disappear down the road followed by little puffs of dust, I pumped some water for the breakfast dishes. When they were washed and dried, I looked around the room. It wasn't so much a matter of what to throw out as what not to throw out. I pitched two orange crates through the door, along with some old newspapers. There was a broom, and I swept out the dust and dried leaves. I pulled the sofa closer to the fireplace and dragged the table and chairs to a window where we could look out at the woods while we ate. The window was so dirty you could barely see through it, so I got some water and a rag and washed it. It was a little streaked when I finished, but it looked better.

The worst thing was the spiders. The whole house was swathed in webs. Every kind of spider seemed to live there, tan ones with great long delicate legs, and black ones with thick bodies and hooked legs, and gray ones that were nearly invisible in their webs. I had the feeling if I didn't keep moving tiny footprints would inch up my leg and sticky threads would wrap themselves all around me.

I wandered into my bedroom to put my clothes away. The first dresser drawer I opened had a pile of cottony fluff in one corner. When I looked more closely

I could see pink things in the middle of the fluff. They were alive. I shut the drawer and stood there, my heart pounding. After a few minutes my curiosity got the better of me, and I opened the drawer a few inches. The pink things were about the size of my little fingernail. They had big heads and long tails and their eyes were closed. They were baby mice. I considered dumping out the drawer in the yard. I didn't want to share my dresser with a family of mice. But they were so young, they wouldn't survive without their mother. I got a few bread crumbs, dropped them in the drawer, and carefully shut it.

The rest of the drawers were pleasantly empty and I arranged my clothes in neat piles, telling myself all the while that in six months' time the clothes would be repacked. When I had finished, I felt a little better about the house. With all the arranging and putting away, it was mine now. It's hard to completely hate something that belongs to you.

When he got back, my father looked around approvingly. "Aunt Marcia would be proud of you," he said. "However, I rescued these two solid-mahogany early-Chippendale bookcases you threw out. Nothing but the best for my books." He had an orange crate in each hand.

"And I have some new screening for your window. Also an imported hand-embroidered Madeira tablecloth." He unrolled a length of plastic. "Please note the exquisitely subtle pattern of orange and purple roses. All they had.

"Let's try the electricity." He pulled a chain attached to a light bulb that hung in the middle of the kitchen.

The bulb lighted. "How about the refrigerator?" We listened. It was making a hiccuping hum. I opened the door. It was all green fuzz inside and it smelled.

"Just what I've always wanted," Father said, "a fur-lined icebox." We were cleaning it out when we heard a knock at the front door. At my father's invitation a woman walked in carrying something on a plate, three small children trailing at her heels.

"I'm Mrs. Rachett. We live down the road. Heard they finally found someone to buy the place and then we saw smoke coming out the chimney and figured you had moved in."

One of the seams in the woman's dress was split and a pocket hung by a thread. The children all looked about five years old. Their hair was stringy and uncut and their clothes so mixed up you couldn't tell if they were girls or boys. There were smears of chocolate across their mouths and their noses were running.

"These are my kids. This here is Pam and this is Windell and over there is Calvin." She gave each one a push as she introduced them. The sound of their names seemed to scare them because they hid behind her, punching one another for the best place. "Cut it out," she said. With a quick sidestep she left them all exposed to plain view. They gave her a reproachful look.

"I'm Reverend Lothrop," Father said, "and this is *my* daughter, Clair." The emphasis on "my" made me furious. As though I were on the same level with those dirty, snotty-nosed brats.

"So you're a reverend. What you doing living here?"

"I hope to start up a little mission church. I was told there might be a need for one."

"Well, you won't find anyone around here with money to build you a church, if that's what you're after."

"As a matter of fact I thought we might have our meetings in my home for a while."

"That your car out there?" she asked.

"Yes."

She gave him a sly glance. "Looks like you been doing pretty good where you was. What you want to come here for? Your wife probably won't like this house too much. Even our house can beat it and that's not saying much."

"My wife died a few months ago."

The woman's face softened and the three children who had been jumping on the davenport, one to a cushion, stopped and looked solemnly at me as if I were some kind of orphan freak.

"I'm sorry to hear that," the woman said. She held the plate out to me. There was a lopsided cake on it. The chocolate frosting was covered with fingerprints. "Here's your dessert for tonight."

My father hurried to cover up for my not saying anything. "That's really very kind of you, Mrs. Rachett. It's reassuring to know we have such thoughtful neighbors. We're looking forward to enjoying the peace and quiet you have up here."

"Don't count on that, Reverend. Just last night they dragged Thorn Norcher outa his house not more 'n a mile or two from you and put him in jail. He tried to set fire to a bar because they wouldn't serve him no more to drink and then he come on home and probably would have beat on his girl like he used to beat on his wife when she was alive, only the sheriff got there first."

Father looked startled. "Where's his daughter now?"

"Guess she's with her grandmother, but I don't know that she'll stay there. She's run away before. Got a mind of her own. Well, I better be getting." She yanked the children one by one off the couch. "Nice meeting you, Reverend," she said, and then she turned to me. "You do any baby-sitting?"

I looked at the three grubby children, the smallest of whom seemed to be in the process of wetting his pants. I shook my head firmly.

"Perhaps Clair can teach them in our Sunday school one day," my father said.

I shot him a killing glance.

When they left I ran into my bedroom, slamming the door behind me, and flung myself down on the bed. What would I do for friends? Would I be shut up here with my crazy father for six months? I'd be bored to death. I swore I'd stay in my room until I rotted. Or maybe I'd run away like the girl that woman had been talking about. I had walked over to the window with some idea of crawling out, when I saw something hanging like an acrobat from the curtain rod. It was an upside-down mouse. Then I saw it had wings that were wrapped around its small body like someone trying to keep warm. One eye slowly opened and looked at me. I ran out of the room. Rotting in a room was one thing. Rotting in a room with a bat was something else.

We worked all week to get the house ready for Sunday's church service. My father borrowed folding chairs from the local undertaker, who also ran the small hardware store in town. "I expect anyone sitting on chairs from a funeral parlor will maintain a certain dignified decorum during services," he said, grinning at the SIMP-SON'S FUNERAL HOME sign printed in big black letters on the back of each chair. "Certainly it's a reminder of where we're all headed. The chairs will say it better than I can."

When Sunday came I was disgusted to see the Rachetts trooping in with their three children. Mr. Rachett was a tall, thin, hollow-cheeked man with droopy eyelids and jowls like a hound dog's. He looked like gravity pulled at him harder than it did at other people. The Rachetts made for the front row, as if it were the best seat in the house, which just went to show how little they knew. In Westville Heights people would have died rather than sit in the front row of the church.

As soon as the Rachetts' children found out the chairs folded, they tried to fold themselves up in them. Finally their parents started passing them back and forth to keep them quiet. It looked like a football game.

The Simpsons were there, too. I could see my father considered this a good sign. I thought maybe they had just come to keep an eye on their chairs. "Used to drive to the next town for church and never could get back in time to get out to the lake before the sun was high and the fish had stopped bitin'," Mr. Simpson said. "Don't know if you're any good, Reverend, but you can't be worse than that fellow in Lakecrest. He mumbles into his beard so you can't hardly understand a word he says, and when you make the effort it isn't worth it. In my business you get to hear plenty of preachers, and I consider I'm something of a judge."

Mrs. Simpson looked around our small house. "Well,

you've settled in pretty well considering what you got to work with."

"I hope you're not going to talk politics," Mr. Simpson said, interrupting his wife. "I hate to hear politics from the pulpit. Leave politics to the devil, I say." Then he sat down on one of his chairs.

It looked like no one else would come, but a minute or two before the service started, a girl about my age slipped in the door, gave a quick look around the room, and took a chair in the back row. She had sun-streaked brown hair cut in uneven lengths like a dress whose hem dipped. Her arms and legs were tan, and so was part of her face, but the top half of her forehead was pale white, as though she didn't often brush her hair back. I noticed her quick brown eyes took everything in without getting caught up in anyone else's glance. Her clothes were neat, but one sleeve of her T-shirt had a large round hole and there was another hole just like it in one of the legs of her slacks.

When the Rachetts and Simpsons saw her, they gave each other funny looks. The girl noticed and sank deeper into her seat. She held the hymnal up in front of her face, mouthing the words, but I could tell no sound was coming out, even though it was a hymn just about everyone knew.

When it came time for the sermon, my father made a big business of taking off his wristwatch and putting it in front of him on the pulpit (the wooden crates covered with a sheet). I saw Mr. Simpson's shoulders heave at the sight of the wristwatch. He let out a big sigh that everyone could hear. But the sermon turned out to be short.

My father talked about how lucky we all were to

be so close to nature where God spoke to us in so many voices. I thought if God was going to speak to me with bats and mice I wasn't sure I wanted to listen. At the end of the service I started toward the girl, but before I could make my way across the room she disappeared through the door. Mrs. Rachett watched her go. "I don't know what that girl is thinking about coming here. You see her sneak out? She's got her dad's ways for sure."

"Who is she?" my father asked.

"Dorrie Norcher. Her dad's that Thorn Norcher I was telling you about. Drove his wife to the grave with his meanness. Dorrie must have come over from her grandma's."

"Where is the Norcher house?"

"Down by Miller Pond off Three Mile Road."

"She knows how to fish, that girl," Mr. Simpson said. "I've seen her take a perch out of Miller Pond that would feed two people. Which reminds me, we got to be on our way if I'm going to do any good in the lake today." He turned to my father. "You kept the service good and short," he said. "And you didn't mumble. I'll spread the word."

❧ SIX

The next morning my father decided he would make some calls. "I think it would be friendly to give folks a personal invitation to worship with us. Let them see what a handsome, clean-cut fellow I am. You don't mind being alone for a while?"

I shook my head. And it was true. I wasn't afraid to stay by myself anymore. The woods behind our house no longer seemed to move toward me when I looked the other way. Besides, I had plans.

As soon as Father left, I got out the township map he had been studying and took it into my room along with a piece of cheese for the dresser-drawer mice. They had brown fur now and would nibble cheese from my hand. Their small flower-petal ears were rimmed with white and their whiskers tickled my fingers.

The map was divided into sections. Each section, Father had explained, was a square mile. Scattered over the squares were small dots that showed where the houses were. There was even a dot for our stone house so we knew we were really there. Miller Pond looked like it was about a mile and a half away from us. I put an apple in my pocket in case I got hungry and left a note for my father so he would know where I was going. I thought it was eerie that the first girl my age I had seen up north had also lost her mother. That might have been what made me want to meet her. But what would she think about my not talking?

Three Mile Road sort of petered out into a dirt track that ran along an open field and then disappeared into the woods. Once I was in the woods it was like walking through a dark tunnel and not knowing what might be on the other side. I told myself I would go a little way and see how it felt. I could always turn back. I found I was nearly running and made myself slow down because the faster I walked the more it felt as though someone were behind me. Once I stopped to look at a pine tree, no taller than my finger. Another time I gathered a handful of acorns — for their shape or their shiny brown color or because they felt smooth in my hand.

I had begun to wonder if I'd lost my way when I saw a patch of blue through the trees, and in another minute I came out at the pond. It was about the size of a very small lake. Across the pond from where I was standing was thick woods. In front of me was a house. Well, not exactly a house. A chimney stuck up from what looked like an underground cellar. It was a room sunk into the ground. Near the cellar entrance a goat stood munching on a tuft of grass. The goat swung its head up, looked at me briefly, and returned to its meal.

There was junk everywhere: old tin pails, tires, bottles, bicycle parts, and a lot of old lumber. Except it was organized into neat piles, so that maybe it wasn't junk after all.

A door on the top of the cellar opened, and the girl from church stuck her head out. For a minute I thought she was going to disappear back into the cellar, but then she opened the door a bit wider, came out, and jumped down to the ground. She was wearing the same clothes she had in church, but now her other sleeve had a hole. "What you got there?" she asked.

I held up the acorns.

"You can grind them up for flour," she said. "If the oven worked I could show you how to make bread from them. You're the minister's daughter. I saw you Sunday." She waited for me to answer. When I didn't, she looked kind of puzzled and went on. "I'm Dorrie Norcher but I suppose you already heard that from the people in church. They don't know how to mind their own business." She saw me steal a glance at the goat. "Come and meet Guinevere. I named her after King Arthur's queen. She belonged to my mother. Now she's mine. I get milk from her and I know how to make cheese from it." Dorrie walked over to the goat. I trailed along behind her.

The goat was black with floppy silver ears and a silver muzzle. Its pink lips turned up at the corners in a foolish smile. But the strange thing about the goat was its eyes. They were like amber beads with shiny black pupils, and the pupils, instead of being round, were shaped like dashes.

Dorrie rubbed her face against the goat's furry neck.

The goat turned its head and nuzzled her back, gently licking her face and pulling at her shirt with small white teeth. When Dorrie stood up, I saw the goat had a piece of her T-shirt in its mouth and was thoughtfully chewing on it.

"Oh, you dumbbell!" Dorrie yelled at the goat. "It's not her fault," she explained. "If I could buy her the grain she's supposed to have, she wouldn't do that. You can pet her if you want to."

I reached over and patted the goat, keeping a careful distance from her mouth. She felt soft and bony at the same time. I took the apple out of my pocket and looked toward the goat. Dorrie stared such a long time at the apple I wished I had offered it to her instead of the goat. Finally she said, "Go ahead and give it to Guinevere." As we watched the goat crunch the apple between its sharp teeth, Dorrie asked, "Don't you talk?"

I shook my head.

"That's all right," Dorrie said. "Neither does Guinevere, and we get along fine. You want to come fishing with me?"

I nodded, relieved that even though I didn't talk she was still willing to be friends with me.

On the way to the pond, Dorrie stopped to dig some worms. She turned over a shovelful of dirt and quickly reached down to yank at the disappearing tails. "Come here, you guys," she said. They stretched like rubber bands. I looked away.

Dorrie led me to a raft hammered together from logs and old boards. I must have looked doubtful because she was reassuring. "You don't have to worry, I made it myself. Get on and I'll push it out."

I scrambled aboard and sat huddled in the middle of the raft while Dorrie, whose feet were bare, waded out into the water, pulling the raft along with her. When it was floating, she jumped on, nearly turning us over. The raft was attached to what looked like several lengths of clothesline fastened together. The clothesline was tied to the trunk of a birch tree at the edge of the water. When we were free of the shore the raft drifted out to the middle of the pond and bobbed gently at the end of the rope.

Dorrie threaded a hook through a worm like she was making shish kebab and threw her line into the water. It drifted down and disappeared into some sinister-looking weeds. I was sort of holding my breath. Anything could come out of weeds that looked like that. Dorrie's pole arced and she gave it a jerk. There was a lot of thrashing around in the water while a fish was reeled in. It had a white belly and pale lemon stripes on its back. Dorrie grabbed it by the tail and slapped its head hard against the bottom of the raft. The fish gave a feeble twitch and lay still. I winced. "They don't mind," Dorrie reassured me.

While Dorrie fished, I looked around the pond. It was the leafy green color of the trees that surrounded it. Along the shore there was a fringe of tall grasses. Where the water was shallow, lily pads floated as big as dinner plates. Two ducks swam among the pond lilies. One was brown with a white-and-blue patch on its side. The other one had a bright green head and neck. They kept so close to each other they might have been tied together by strings.

Suddenly Dorrie asked, "Does your father raise spirits in his church?"

I looked puzzled.

"I mean can he get dead people to talk?"

I shook my head hard.

"Oh." Dorrie sounded disappointed. "My grandma is a medium. She has these séances (she pronounced it see-ants) where people pay her to let them talk to the dead. Anyhow that's what she says. She won't ever let me watch. She gets all these spooky magazines with names like *Spirit* and *Through the Veil* and *Afterward*. I read them when I stay there. I wanted her to bring back my mother so I could talk to her but she said my mother would only cause trouble for her boy. Her boy is my dad. That's why I came to your church on Sunday. I think my ma might know something that would keep my dad in jail for a long time. If he gets out he'll get drunk and break up everything in our house again."

I guess I must have looked shocked, because Dorrie sort of shrugged. "What can I do? I just take off into the woods for a couple of days and stay in this hideout I made until he sobers up." She pulled in another fish and killed it dead. "I'm supposed to be living with my grandma but she doesn't want me. She's glad when I run away. She doesn't even tell the welfare worker I'm gone because the welfare pays her for keeping me and if they knew I wasn't there she'd lose the money. Don't you tell anyone you saw me here."

I shook my head no, that I wouldn't.

Dorrie said, "I guess you won't. I forgot you can't talk. See, I just want to live here by myself. I can make out all right. Only it would help if I could talk to my ma. Sometimes I almost can even without a séance." I thought of the strange feeling I had the night of the

46

full moon and wished I could have told Dorrie about it.

"Come on, I'll show you my house," Dorrie said. "I've got it all fixed up." She began to pull hand over hand at the rope, gathering it in, until we reached the shore. We climbed off the raft and walked over to the boxed-in doorway that sat like a top hat on the roof of the cellar. A stairway led down to a dark room where only a faint glow of light shone through two small glass-brick windows. The walls of the room were covered with hundreds of pictures cut from magazines, most of them outdoor scenes, as though Dorrie were making up for not being able to look out of a window. There was hardly any furniture around, but there were a lot of knickknacks, quite a few of them broken.

"I can't turn on any lights," Dorrie apologized. "My dad never paid the electric bills and I don't have any money. Sometimes I get the feeling I'm buried alive down here, but one day I'm going to build a sitting room on top of the house with a window big enough to let me watch the pond. There's always something doing there. The deer come down and drink early in the morning and just before dark. There's muskrat, and where the creek flows into the pond there's a beaver house.

"I've got nearly enough lumber for the sitting room. Did you see it piled up outside? I find a lot of good stuff around old broken-down cabins. But the best place is the dump. There're all kinds of things there." She pointed out a china lamp. The shade was a little dented, but otherwise it looked fine. "I got that and a toaster yesterday, but I can't use either of them for now. I get lots of magazines and dishes and pans; even the

47

curtains are from there. I'm going tomorrow. You want to come?"

I nodded. Dorrie made it sound like an enormous department store.

"Care for some milk?" she asked politely.

It was nearly one o'clock and I hadn't had lunch.

She fished a glass jar out of a pail of water and poured some milk into two jelly glasses. "It's from Guinevere."

When I heard that I had to force myself to take a sip. I didn't like the idea of knowing where my milk came from. It was too personal. But the milk was cold and turned out to taste pretty good.

"There's plenty to eat around here," Dorrie told me. "Besides the fish, I go out and gather stuff from the woods." She dipped into the pail again. "Here's marsh marigolds and pond-lily roots and cattails. The cattails don't taste very good but they're pretty. It's like eating corn on the cob made out of green velvet. My ma showed me how you fix all this stuff. Her ma showed her. In a couple of weeks the berries will start. And I eat a lot of fish. That's brain food. You can take the fish I caught home with you."

I shook my head. I figured she needed all the food she could get.

But Dorrie looked hurt. "You take them. I'm going fishing this afternoon, and I'll get as many as I can eat. I can't keep them without a refrigerator anyhow. You could bring me some bread tomorrow, though. If you've got some extra. I can shake up cream in a fruit jar and get butter but I don't have any bread to put it on." She was quiet for a minute. I could see there was something else she wanted. "If you have any cereal like oatmeal or cornflakes, you could bring a little of that too — for Guinevere. All she gets is grass. Too much of that gives her gas." Dorrie wrapped the fish up in some newspapers from the dump and handed them to me.

The walk back went much faster. I recognized things I had noticed on the way to Dorrie's: the small pine, a patch of milky blue flowers, a tree with one branch twisted into a funny shape. It was strange to think that these woods might become as familiar as Westville Heights' streets and houses.

When I got to the stone house I saw an old beat-up car parked in front. It was the kind of car that used to drive through Westville Heights on hot summer nights. I tried to remember what the Rachetts' car had looked like. It seemed to me theirs was newer than that. The car was empty and I wondered how the Rachetts could have gotten into our house. My father wasn't home, because there was no sign of the station wagon. I climbed up the steps slowly. When I looked through the window I was startled to find Father looking out at me. He swung open the front door. "You've been gone a long time. I was just about to start out for the Norchers'."

I handed him the fish, wishing I could tell him all about Dorrie.

"You must have gone fishing at the pond," he said. "I thought the Norcher girl lived at her grandmother's. Is her father back?" I shook my head. "She's not living there alone?" I shook my head again. "Well, I'm glad to hear that. We'd certainly have to notify the authorities if

49

that were the case. Well, then, is her grandmother with her?"

I nodded yes, hoping lies were not quite as bad if you didn't actually say them out loud. Even if they were, I had promised Dorrie I wouldn't give her away. I could see my father believed me, and, since I wasn't that good a liar, I decided he must have something else on his mind. An awful thought occurred to me. I went to the window and pointed to the old car parked in front of our house.

My father wouldn't meet my eyes. "It's *our* car," he said. "I sold the station wagon."

I fought back tears. The blue station wagon was the only link left to Westville Heights.

Looking miserable, he said, "I started out making my calls, but people kept noticing that showy car. I knew they were thinking I was some sort of flim-flam salesman making a fast dollar by hawking the gospel. It just didn't make sense to them, a country preacher with a preten- tious car like that.

"I know you're upset about it, Clair. You think I've broken my promise. I suppose you don't see us driving back to Westville Heights in that jalopy."

I had turned my back to him. I didn't want to give him the satisfaction of seeing me cry.

"I want you to know, Clair, I put the money from the car into the bank. It will stay there. We can always get a new car." He paused. "That is, if you still want to go back when the six months are up."

I shot him an angry look, but I felt a lot better. The money was safe. And my father wasn't asking any more questions about Dorrie.

That night I skipped the peanut-butter sandwich I

usually had before I went to bed and hid two pieces of bread for Dorrie. I knew my father would be suspicious if he saw me taking food along. In the morning I would get up early and sneak some oatmeal for Guinevere. I thought of the goat's gold eyes looking out into the dark. But perhaps she spent the night down in the cellar with Dorrie. I hoped so. I didn't like to think of Dorrie all alone at night in the woods. As I fell asleep I could hear my father as he turned out the lights and shut the windows. It was a comforting sound.

🌿 SEVEN

The next morning I had finished my breakfast and hidden a bag with bread for Dorrie and oatmeal and apples for Guinevere. My father looked surprised to see me ready to leave. "Isn't it a little early to go visiting?" he asked. I think he was pleased, though, to see me enthusiastic about something for a change. "I suppose you and Dorrie are getting in some fishing this morning?"

I just smiled.

Dorrie was milking Guinevere when I got there. The goat's head and neck were stuck in a space between two boards to keep her standing still. I stared fascinated at how quickly Dorrie got the milk out. "I'd let you milk her," Dorrie said, "but she knows my touch. I'm not sure she'd stand still for you."

When the milking was over, I gave Guinevere the oatmeal I had brought. She turned her gold eyes up to me and gave my hand a lick with her rough tongue.

When the oatmeal was gone she snatched at the bag to get the apples. Dorrie pulled it away. "You brought bread," she said, looking inside. "Come on, we'll fix some sandwiches to take to the dump."

Guinevere trotted along behind us, jumping lightly over the piles of lumber. When we went downstairs, the goat followed, taking the stairs two and three at a time. I looked at Dorrie. "She's real good in the house," Dorrie reassured me. "Goats are about the cleanest animals there are. Except billy goats. Ugh! They smell. The Rachetts have one. If you let him stand next to a milking goat the milk will smell.

"I've got watercress for sandwiches," Dorrie said. "It grows in the creek where the beavers are. If you come sometime at night, we can watch the beavers swimming around." Guinevere reached down into the pail and helped herself to the watercress.

I wondered if the goat would go with us to the dump. But she didn't.

"Too much for her to eat there that isn't good for her," Dorrie said.

We could smell the dump long before we got there. The odor was a mixture of burned rubber and decaying garbage. It smelled so awful I hung back. Dorrie noticed and told me not to worry about the smell. "You get used to it. After a while you won't even notice it."

The dump was a huge open ditch full of smoldering tires and rubbish. I was ready to turn around and head back home as fast as possible, when Dorrie ran up to the edge of the ditch and began to pick up bottles and cans and throw them in every direction. I thought she was out of her head.

"Chasing away the rats," she called over her shoulder. There were quick scampering movements around the garbage. Then things were quiet. "Wow, look over there!" Dorrie called and began scrambling down into the ditch. She kicked some cans and paper off an old pink shag rug and dragged it up for me to admire. "It's hardly worn at all. It'll wash up fine and I can put it in the sitting room."

In spite of myself I inched closer to the ditch. I could see the white ghosts of old kitchen appliances and mattresses bleeding their stuffing. The more you looked, the more there was. Dorrie was back down tugging at a bike wheel.

Something blue caught my eye. I put a foot over the edge and cautiously slipped a few feet at a time down the side toward an enameled pitcher that was a lovely spotted blue and white, like clouds across a summer sky. I reached down and picked it up with two fingers, holding it away from me to let a trickle of dirty water drip out. Apart from a small chip on the handle it was in perfect condition.

"Give me a hand," Dorrie was calling. I helped her dig out a folding lawn chair. It had a wooden frame and a faded green-and-red-striped canvas seat with a long tear down the center. Dorrie said she could mend it. "It'll be nice for under the tree in the yard. I can sit there in the afternoon and have refreshments." The way she talked it sounded like the pictures you see of Victorian ladies in their gardens drinking tea from little china cups. "There's a lot I could take back if I had something to carry it away in," Dorrie said. I thought wistfully of how much the station wagon could have held.

We found an earring made out of a shell, a geranium plant that wasn't dead, a mirror with just one small crack, some aluminum pie tins, and lots of wire hangers and magazines. At noon we stopped to eat our lunch of watercress sandwiches. They tasted crisp and peppery, but I would rather have had peanut butter.

The odor from the dump didn't bother me anymore. Even the rats that had crept silently back to forage in the rubbish didn't seem so bad. We had had our turn; now it was theirs.

"I found some old snowshoes here once," Dorrie said between bites. "I'll let you use them this winter." I shook my head.

Dorrie looked puzzled, then disappointed. "You going back to the city?" I nodded. "What do you want to do that for? I wouldn't live in the city for anything. I'd sooner live with my grandma and her cats, and that's saying something. She's got about fifty cats in her house, and if you complain when they use your bed for a bathroom, she gets furious. The cats get liver and all I get is scalloped potatoes. And the house smells, and when the welfare lady is supposed to come to see if I'm getting taken care of, my grandma puts all the cats in boxes and ties them up with string and pokes holes in the boxes so the darn cats can breathe. Then she puts them in her car and drives it away and parks it so you can't hear the cats yowling. After the lady goes, she brings the cats back and lets them out. They just about climb the walls and they claw and scratch you. She has to cut the strings on the boxes and then we stand back. She says cats are witchy and keep bad spirits away."

An old truck rattled to a stop a few feet from us,

showering us with sand. A man got out, let down the tailgate, and started throwing out plastic bags filled with trash. We watched the cans and garbage shoot out of the open bags, hoping for something useful. The man threw out a rusted fire extinguisher. Dorrie was only mildly interested. Then he was lifting out something heavy and pushing it over the edge. A wheelbarrow!

As soon as he had driven off, we flew down the side of the dump, the soft sand crumbling under our feet. We each grabbed a handle of the wheelbarrow and began to tug, bumping it along through the trash. With a final heave we eased it over the side of the ditch onto the road. The front wheel was wobbly and the bottom of the barrow was a little rusted out; otherwise it was in good shape. We piled our finds into it and pushed it triumphantly down the road. "Now we can get the rest of the lumber for my sitting room," Dorrie said. "If you help me we can have it built by fall before you have to go away."

❧ EIGHT

When we got back to the pond, Dorrie sewed up the chair seat while I gathered flowers to put in my blue pitcher. Dorrie said they were field daisies and hawkweed. As I was arranging the flowers, she asked in a whisper if I would like to see her secret hideout.

I nodded.

"I wouldn't show it to anyone else," she said, "but since you can't talk I guess you'd keep it a secret." She untied Guinevere's rope and the two of us followed her to the creek that flowed into the pond and then along a small feeder brook that led through the woods. The goat seemed pleased at the idea of a walk, hopping along and sort of kicking its heels and making little bleating noises. Every once in a while she would stop to graze. Once Dorrie yanked her away from something. "Bracken fern," she said. "That's poison for goats."

"It's not the only reason I keep her on a rope, though. My dad's got traps set all through here. He traps anything bigger than a mouse — raccoon, fox, muskrat, beaver. He sells the skins.

"It wouldn't be so bad if he'd go around and get the animals right away, but he gets drunk and forgets where he put the traps. Then the animals just die by inches. He's got traps out now, but I've sprung all the ones I could find. When he comes out and sees what I've done, he'll be mad as the devil.

"He's just about the only one who can find his way through these woods." She sounded almost proud of him. "I've gotten lost a couple of times. When you're walking you have to watch and see where the sun is. Then if you know what time it is you can tell east and west."

The brook disappeared underground, and the earth became soft and spongy. The trees had changed from maple and birch to a matted tangle of evergreens. "Tamarack and cedar," Dorrie said. "The deer come here in the wintertime." She stopped to tie Guinevere up. "Gets too wet for her."

The swamp had a shipwrecked look. Trees grew at odd angles like tilted masts. I didn't like the place. When you put your foot down you didn't know if the ground would hold you or if your foot would sink into the pools of black water. The branches snapped back at you in an angry way. Overhead the sun was shining, but only a little of it got through the thick canopy of branches. I was wondering how I could let Dorrie know that I wanted to turn back, when I looked up to find her gone. I would have turned and run, but I didn't know which way to go.

I heard Dorrie laugh. "Over here!" I followed the sound of her voice and saw her stick her head out of a

58

sort of teepee made of fir branches. It was so cleverly hidden I could have walked by it a dozen times without noticing it. Dorrie said, "I told you it was a good hiding place. I can get water from the pools and these cedars are so thick no one could ever find me. Once my dad got close enough for me to touch him and he never saw me. You want to come in?"

An old plastic sheet had been laid over the thick layer of cedar branches that made up the floor. On top of the plastic Dorrie had spread some old blankets. "I could stay here for days," Dorrie said. "There's an open space not far from here where I can get all the berries I want. I call it the berry bowl. My dad traps there a lot. The grouse come and eat the berries and the foxes come and eat them. My dad goes after the foxes.

"If you ever hear my dad's out of jail," Dorrie said in a serious voice, "you could look for me here. Only you'd have to be sure no one followed you."

A second after she said that, something came running through the woods and rushed at the teepee. I held my breath, but it was only Guinevere, who had chewed through her rope. She butted her head affectionately against Dorrie. Dorrie put an arm around the goat's long neck. "Darn dumbbell," she said.

Going back, Dorrie warned me to stay close to her. "It's easy to get lost. There was this boy hunting deer here two years ago and he never came out. They had to wait to find his body until the snow melted in the spring. My dad led the search party. When he came back he said that would happen to me if I didn't stay out of the woods. He didn't want me to find out he was trapping out of season.

"Here's where I know to turn." She pointed to a large gray beech tree that looked like an elephant's foot. Just beyond the tree I saw a slight movement in the bracken. Dorrie saw it too. As we got closer we could hear faint whistling sounds. A brown animal about the size of a kitten sat up on its hind feet and peered at us. "It's a woodchuck," Dorrie said. There was a steel trap beside it. The teeth of the trap were fastened around the leg of a dead animal. Why hadn't the woodchuck the sense to run as far as possible from the trap? After just a glance I couldn't even bring myself to look at it, but Dorrie poked around at the dead animal. "Probably its mother," she said. "She must have died of thirst. Sometimes they bite their legs off to get free." Dorrie knew some really grisly things.

She pointed to a hollow dug into the roots of a nearby tree. "My dad must have thought it was a foxhole. Woodchuck skins aren't worth anything." The baby woodchuck still hadn't moved. "I guess we better take it before one of the foxes gets it. You want to carry it?" She knew I did.

I scooped it up, surprised at how small its body was beneath its thick coat. I had never seen a wild animal up that close. The fur on its back was a warm brown, shading into rusty orange on its stomach. Its ears were round, and it had long white teeth with the kind of overbite that would have thrilled my Uncle Keith. The woodchuck dug its head into the crook of my elbow and stayed perfectly still on the trip back. It was strange holding something wild like that. It was as if one of us had crossed an invisible barrier.

When we got the woodchuck back to the pond

Dorrie gathered some plantain leaves for it. It wouldn't eat them, so we got the idea of giving him some of Guinevere's milk with an eyedropper. When it had had as much as it wanted, it lay on its back, paws up in the air, and went to sleep. It was a male woodchuck.

"What'll we call him?" Dorrie asked. She was thoughtful about asking my advice even though I never said anything. Or maybe that's why she always asked. "We'll call him Percival," she decided. When Dorrie had first started going to the dump she had found a book about King Arthur. Besides Guinevere and Percival, Dorrie had named the two ducks on the pond Elaine and Lancelot, and there was a kingfisher she called Galahad.

When the woodchuck woke up he ambled over to where Guinevere was. At first the goat did a lot of bleating and made some butting motions, but the woodchuck wasn't scared. It started to chew on some clover right under Guinevere's nose. Guinevere lowered her head and opened her mouth. We ran toward them, thinking she was going to take a bite out of Percival. Instead, she started to lick him with her rough tongue, knocking him over about a dozen times in the process. Percival just kept on eating, and he never stopped all the rest of the summer.

NINE

More and more people came trooping to the services at our house on Sundays. When the Simpson Funeral Home chairs started to creep onto the front porch and into the kitchen, my father began to look around for a permanent place for a church. He pretty much left me to myself, never asking questions about my daily visits to Dorrie's except to wonder occasionally if Dorrie's grandmother wasn't getting a little tired of having me there so often. I could see he was relieved to have me occupied and not moping around the house the way I had in Westville Heights.

Although he never said anything about my not talk-ing, I'd catch him watching me in a sad, puzzled way. When I saw how unhappy it made him it was hard not to say something. But I was sure if I did, I'd never get back to Westville Heights. He'd believe our new life up north had cured me. The worst times for him were when we were invited out to other people's houses.

Like the time the Simpsons had us over. I wasn't too happy about eating dinner in an undertaker's house but it turned out to be a sort of cheerful place, with so many fluffy white hand-crocheted doilies scattered around on the tables and furniture it looked like it had been snowing inside. Except I was afraid to go to the bathroom for fear I would open the wrong door and see something awful.

Anyhow, the Simpsons must have heard about my not talking because all the questions they directed to me were what my English teacher used to call rhetorical. Like Mrs. Simpson would say, "Well, Clair, you've gotten yourself a real tan, haven't you?" Or, "Don't you think you could eat just one more of these nice home-baked brownies, Clair?" Even if I could have talked a blue streak I wouldn't have had to open my mouth to answer imbecile questions like that.

It embarrassed Father to have people treat me like I wasn't all there. I think he wished they'd lose patience with me and just shake me until some words started to come out. Sometimes he looked like that's what *he* wanted to do. But of course he didn't.

Dorrie was never bothered by my silence. She talked enough for the two of us. We were spending our mornings scrounging lumber for the sitting room. Next to the dump the best places were abandoned shacks along Three Mile Road where the old lumber camps used to be. Over the years the shacks had fallen apart, and all Dorrie had to do was take her dad's crowbar and pry the boards apart and then we'd load them on our wheelbarrow. The valuable lumber had long since been carried away. What was left was weathered and full of knotholes, but Dorrie said we could nail our aluminum pie tins over the holes.

Once we found a whole door with the handle still on it. All it lacked was hinges. Our best discovery, though, was a window. When you looked through it everything was a little wavy; the top part of what you saw didn't quite match the bottom. But none of the glass was broken.

When we got it back to the pond we carried it up to the cellar roof and spent the afternoon moving it around to see what the best view would be. One of us would steady it while the other one stood back and looked through it.

I thought we ought to put the window so we could see the north end of the pond where the creek and the beavers were, but Dorrie wanted to be able to see the road. "If my dad comes down that road I've got to have enough time to take off."

One afternoon a car did appear. "Oh, Lord," Dorrie said, "it's my grandma." Dorrie's grandmother didn't look like any grandmother I had ever seen. She had hair so black it looked as if it were painted on her head and she wore lots of green eyeshadow. She had tacky glasses with little diamonds on them and skin-tight slacks. "Well, you got yourself a little friend," she said to Dorrie. She looked at me suspiciously. "I suppose she's told everyone you're living here by yourself. Next thing the welfare will be stopping their checks."

"Clair can't talk," Dorrie told her.

"Ain't that kind of strange," her grandmother said. Then she seemed to forget I was there. "Your dad's going to be getting out one of these days and he'll blow his top if he sees all this old junk around his house. I can't figure out what a son of mine was doing living in a godforsaken place like this anyhow. I suppose it was your ma's idea. She thought she could change your dad by hiding him here in the woods. You might as well pour perfume on a pig. He'd find himself a drink in the middle of the Sahara. What in heaven's name is that?" Percival came waddling out of the woods. He stood up on his hind feet and peered at Mrs. Norcher.

"That's Percival," Dorrie said. "He's a woodchuck."

"He looks like some kind of rat to me."

Percival walked over to Guinevere and began nibbling on the outer edge of her patch of dandelions.

"Between that smelly goat and that rodent this place is a regular zoo," Mrs. Norcher said.

"Guinevere doesn't smell. Anyhow, what about all your cats?"

"Don't you sass me." Mrs. Norcher headed for the house. "Ain't you going to invite me in?" She didn't wait for an answer, but just walked over to the entrance to the cellar and started down the steps. We followed after her. "Well, you got some new stuff since I was here last. Where'd that rug come from?"

"I found it at the dump," Dorrie told her.

"That's a filthy place. You could catch germs there." She picked up a movie magazine and began to flick through it. "Somebody once took me for Elizabeth Taylor," she said and gave her black hair a pat. Putting the magazine down, she strutted over to the kitchen. "What you eatin' these days?"

"Clair brings me bread and I catch fish and make cheese."

"What are these?" Dorrie's grandmother poked at

some milkweed buds we had gathered. Dorrie boiled them on an outdoor fire and they tasted like broccoli, only not as serious. "You still eatin' stuff from the woods? It'll poison you one day. It probably killed your ma. There's a lot of difference between a deer's or a goat's stomach and a person's. They spit their food up and then spend all day chewing it. A person doesn't do that."

"My mother died because my dad kept telling her she wasn't sick and she didn't need a doctor." Dorrie's face was working to keep from crying; at the same time she looked furious.

"Thorn's no angel, but he's still my son, and I won't hear that kind of talk against him. You say things like that and I'll make the welfare send you to the training school for running away from me." Her grandmother was screeching.

"Then you won't get your check for me each month," Dorrie shouted back.

"What do I care about that lousy check! It hardly keeps the cats in food."

But Mrs. Norcher had stopped yelling. "I got to be going. You probably seen these." She scooped up the movie magazines. She took the pink rug, too. "The cats ruined my bedroom rug. You can find yourself another one next time you go ragpicking."

"Old bitch," Dorrie said under her breath.

Mrs. Norcher didn't hear her.

On warm afternoons when it was too hot to scrounge wood we sat at the edge of the pond, our feet stretched out into the cool water, chewing wild mint and eating hermits. Hermits were the cookies Mrs. Rachett brought over to my father and me once a week. They were so hard we had to dip them in the pond water before we could chew them. Hermits had a lot of oatmeal in them, though, and they were Guinevere's favorites. She could eat them without dipping.

Percival would lie down near us, front and back paws stretched out so he looked like a small rug. There were ten ducks now, Elaine and Lancelot and their eight ducklings. The father scouted good places for the family to eat, then the mother and her ducklings would come sweeping in so close together they looked like one big duck. While the ducklings fed, heads down in the water, tails up, the mother kept watch, her head turning first one way and then another. When she was sure everything was safe, she would snatch a few bites for herself before she rounded up the ducklings and led them away.

When it was hot we'd go swimming in the pond. At first I was leery of stepping into the soft muck on the pond's bottom. You could see snails and clams moving around there. The worst were the crayfish that scuttled along. They were bluish white with long pincers and looked to me like a dead man's hand.

We'd float on our backs looking up at the sky, blue and red dragonflies like bits of colored thread darting over our heads, and from the top of the birch tree the kingfisher making a rackety sound. It was on one of those afternoons that Dorrie announced she was ready to start building the sitting room.

TEN

Each time Dorrie and I wheeled some old hunks of lumber back to the pond I would find myself wondering how we would get the room built. I think I had some wild idea that at just the right moment Dorrie would snap her fingers and all the lumber would spring up and arrange itself into a sitting room, like Joshua tumbling the walls of Jericho only just the opposite.

It wasn't like that. Dorrie had found a book at the dump on how to build a house. It was called *Raising the Roof.* She carried it around with her all the time and a lot of her conversation was about headers and studs and joists. I didn't understand any of it, but it sounded convincing. The only trouble was that when it came time to build we didn't have the right pieces of wood to do what the book said, so we had to make things up as we went along. Our efforts sometimes looked a little strange to me and I worried that the whole thing would fall down, but Dorrie said it was only a matter of using enough nails. I thought it was like fastening the seam of a dress with safety pins; it stayed together, but you knew there was a better way.

Our pieces of wood were different heights and we didn't have a saw. Dorrie said that was no problem. "We'll put the shortest ones first. It'll give us a sloping roof but that's all right. It's more contemporary." It worked except for the fact that after we put the roof on the room you could only stand upright in the back half of it. "Doesn't make any difference," Dorrie said. "It's a sitting room isn't it?"

The closer we came to finishing the room, the harder we worked. Dorrie's thumb was black and blue where she hit it over and over with the hammer, and I had slivers in nearly all my fingers and a sunburned back and more freckles than I had ever had in my life.

Nailing the window into place was the hardest part. We finally attached one side of the window frame to a board and then nailed that board to one of the planks that made up the wall. The window was a little low because of what Dorrie rather grandly called "structural reasons." You got the best view by sitting on the floor. But once the window was in and some big pieces of plywood we had found at the dump nailed on to make the roof, the empty space suddenly became a real room.

Because the paint cans we found at the dump never had more than a little paint left in them, each wall of the sitting room was a different color: green, white, yellow, and orange. It looked a little startling, but it was cheerful. Dorrie had the great idea of hanging the mirror across from the window so it was like having two windows. We didn't have much furniture, but Dorrie said around Labor Day when the women began to house-clean they pitched out a lot of good things. You had to take them away fast, she said, because their husbands sometimes came to the dump and tried to get them back.

The only part we hadn't been able to complete was the door. We couldn't find hinges for it, so we hung an old shower curtain over the entrance. The curtain had silver seashells all over it. Dorrie said they glowed in the dark.

When it rained we stayed inside reading old magazines and looking out the window at the ducks floating on the pond. Guinevere would be there with us because her lean-to leaked and our sitting room was wrapped all over like a Christmas present with scraps of tar paper and not a drop of rain came in. We felt snug sitting there with the quick sound of raindrops on the tar-paper roof and Guinevere nibbling contentedly on the fringe of another rug we had found at the dump to take the place of the one Dorrie's grandmother had carried away.

Dorrie would talk about how she planned to get a job, maybe as a waitress, maybe at a gas station, so she could make enough money to buy trout fingerlings. Those were small trout. You could buy hundreds of them cheap, Dorrie said. "When they get large enough I can charge people to come here and catch them. Then I'd be earning my own living and nobody could make me leave here."

While we were building the sitting room, my father was looking for a place for a church. One day when I came home from Dorrie's, he told me he had found it.

"It's not true Gothic, Clair. No flying buttresses, no vaulting ribs, no carvings and crockets, but we do have a nicely peaked roof and the windows are quite colorful with some fine decorations: two jack-o-lanterns and four snowflakes, to be exact."

After supper he took me to see it. It was an old one-room schoolhouse. The paint was peeling and the snowflakes and pumpkins pasted on the windows were yellow and curled up on the edges. He said it hadn't been used for years, but when you walked inside you almost felt like the class had just been dismissed. A big old clock was still on the wall, and in the cloakroom a knitted cap hung from a hook, and a mitten lay on the floor. I thought it would make a fine church.

"Mrs. Rachett and Mrs. Simpson and the rest of the women in the congregation are going to clean things up and the gentlemen have agreed to do some painting. No Last Judgment on the ceiling or anything like that, you understand, just a little latex in a neutral color."

After we had looked around, Father cleared his throat a couple of times. "There's something I want to talk to you about, Clair."

My heart jumped. I was afraid he had heard that Dorrie was staying by herself and I wouldn't be able to go there anymore. But that wasn't it.

"Even with all the help the congregation has offered, there are going to be expenses. Of course the property itself is cheap. It's been going begging for a long time and we can manage the small monthly mortgage payments from our collection. But there's a down payment of two thousand dollars which I feel ought to be my responsibility. The only way I could put my hands on that kind of money would be to use part of the savings from the sale of the station wagon. I could withdraw what I need for the down payment and still have enough to buy a car to take us back to Westville Heights — that is, if you decide you want to go — but it wouldn't be nearly as grand a car as the station wagon was. What do you say?"

I had never seen my father as excited about anything as he was about the old schoolhouse. He wasn't nearly as enthusiastic when they built the new parish house in Westville Heights with all the meeting rooms and the trustees' room with the long rosewood conference table and the new kitchen with a ten-minute dishwasher and the parking lot for five hundred cars with lots of room between the spaces because there were so many accidents on Sunday when people ran into each other in their hurry to get away from church.

I nodded, glad that the money was all he wanted and that he hadn't found out how Dorrie was living all alone. But a week later he did find out.

❧ ELEVEN

It happened because Dorrie asked me to come and spend the night with her. "We could watch the beavers," she said. She wrote a note in ink to my father inviting me and signed her grandmother's name.

My father said I could go. I don't think he would have been so quick to say yes if his mind hadn't been on his new church. He did suggest that I ought to take a little something with me to show my appreciation to Dorrie's grandmother for her hospitality. "Are Mrs. Rachett's hermits all gone?"

I nodded. Guinevere had eaten the last one that afternoon. He looked in the French cookbook. We were always looking in it but we never made any of the recipes. That was because they called for things like capers and truffles and anchovy butter and a lot of other stuff they didn't have at the local store. "How about *Cornets de Nougat à la Creme?*" my father asked. "Or *Pruneaux aux Farcis Tourangelle?*" We settled on peanut-butter fudge.

He stood at the stove stirring, an old bath towel wrapped around his waist. "I am brought low, indeed. If only the Board of Trustees of the Westville Heights United Church could see what their pastor has come to." He let the fudge overcook and we had to chip it out of the pan with a screwdriver, but it tasted good.

Dorrie and I ate most of it while we were waiting for the sun to set. When it was nearly dark we walked over to the creek. Dorrie said that once it had been only a few feet wide and shallow, but over the years the beavers had built a dam across it and the dam had backed up the water to make the pond. While the pond was quiet and its water too dark to let you see much of what went on in it, the creek kept moving and you could look right down through clear water to the sandy bottom. There were some days when all you wanted was the quiet of the pond. Other days you felt like watching the scramble of the creek.

Below the dam, half in and half out of the creek, was a beaver house nearly fifteen feet across and as tall as I was. Since beavers don't usually come out during the daytime I had never seen one, but Dorrie and I had climbed up on top of their house and heard faint gnawing noises and smelled their animal odor. Their house wasn't a whole lot different from the sitting room. Where we had pieced the sitting room together with scraps of lumber, they had pieced their house together by mounding up branches they had cut from alder bushes and poplar trees. We had weatherproofed the sitting room with tar paper; they weatherproofed their house with mud. As far as neatness was concerned, I think they had the edge.

74

We hid on the bank behind an alder bush. On either side of us were bare stretches of land where the beavers had cut down the dozens of poplars that would feed them all through the winter. The sun had fallen below the row of trees that marked the beginning of the woods. "We have to stay perfectly quiet," Dorrie whispered.

About the time I didn't think I could sit still any longer, the head of a big beaver popped up through the water not far from its house. As it swam along, all you could see was the top of its head and its back. After a while the beaver climbed up on the bank and began running a hind foot through its water-slicked fur. Dorrie whispered that it was spreading oil over its coat so that it would shed water. A second, smaller beaver came out, followed by two beaver kits. They swam upstream, making one large and two small silver triangles of wake. When they reached the shore, they hurried off into the woods. The large beaver followed them. After a while the big beaver returned carrying a piece of tree in his mouth. A few minutes later the smaller beaver and the kits were back, little packets of twigs and leaves in their front paws. They sat on the bank of the creek, stuffing the leaves and twigs into their mouths.

We watched until a damp chill began to rise from the water. "Let's go back," Dorrie said. As soon as he saw us stand up, the big beaver slapped the water with his flat tail, making a noise like an explosion. The smaller beaver and the two kits dove into the water and disappeared. The large beaver swam out toward the middle of the pond and circled around, never taking his eyes off us. "I could get a lot of money for their skins," Dorrie said, "but I'd as soon trap Guinevere."

We were climbing into the sitting room when a pair of headlights picked us out of the darkness. "Come on." Dorrie started to run. "It's my dad." But I recognized the car. It was my own father. He walked over and introduced himself to Dorrie, whereupon Dorrie invited him into the sitting room.

"Uh, is this your home, Dorrie?" There was a look of astonishment on his face.

"My old house is in the cellar. This is where I live now. Clair and I made it." Dorrie was anxious to show the room off. I was uncertain. With my father there I saw it half through Dorrie's eyes and half through his.

"So this is what you've been doing all summer?" he said to me, examining the room. I wished we had found a can of paint large enough to paint the whole room the same color. But he didn't seem to notice the different colors. "I don't know when I've been more impressed," he told us. "You've done . . ." He seemed to be hunting for the right word. ". . . an extraordinary job. It's . . ." He hunted again. ". . . unique."

Dorrie was pleased. "Would you like to sit down?" she asked politely. She pointed out the canvas lawn chair.

Father looked at the gaps in the mended tear and said, "That's kind of you, but I only came to tell your grandmother that I heard your father was going to be released from jail very soon."

Dorrie looked upset.

"By the way, where *is* your grandmother?"

"At the movies," Dorrie said quickly.

"Oh." Father looked puzzled. "Does she often leave you alone like this at night?"

"She'll be back any minute," Dorrie went on coolly.

76

I was nearly convinced myself, except the nearest movie was in a town an hour away. I hoped my father didn't know that.

"I see. Well, I think Clair had better come home with me for tonight. She can stay some other time. Would you like us to wait here with you until your grandmother gets back?"

Dorrie said, "You better not. She'll think you're criticizing her for going out. She hates to be criticized."

Father lifted his eyebrows. "Well, I certainly wouldn't want to give that impression. Perhaps, though, you ought to go down to your 'old' house and lock the door before we leave."

Dorrie promised she would. I followed my father across the yard, worried at how quiet he had become. We were nearly to the car when we saw a black shape run at us. "What the devil's that?" he said. It was Guinevere. I put my arms around the goat and hugged her. Father put a cautious hand on Guinevere's head. She daintily pulled at a piece of yarn on the sleeve of his sweater and began unraveling it. I had to yank it away.

"I see now why you spend so much time with Dorrie," Father said as we drove home. "She seems to lead a most diverting life." A few minutes later he added, "I believe I'll give your Aunt Marcia and Uncle Keith a call tonight. They've taken a place at Blue Harbor for the summer. That's only a couple of hours from here."

I sank down in my seat, thinking nothing good could possibly come of that.

❧ TWELVE

The next morning, before I could get away to Dorrie's, there was a knock at our door. When I went to see who it was I was caught up in my Aunt Marcia's arms. I could smell her familiar perfume. It was like carnations. Then my cheek was against the soft wool of Uncle Keith's jacket. For the first time in weeks I was homesick. Instead of opening a door on the dusty country road I had opened the door to Westville Heights.

"Look at you, Clair," Uncle Keith said, "thin as a reed! But you certainly look healthy. Your father must be feeding you honey and locusts." He laughed and poked me in the belly.

"And you've gone native." Aunt Marcia took in my crumpled T-shirt, my worn cutoffs, and my bare feet.

They looked around at our small house. "This is it?" my uncle asked as though there might be a large and much more suitable house just through a door or behind a wall.

"This is it," Father answered. He sounded defensive.

"I'm sure it's comfortable," my aunt said quickly. "It definitely has possibilities. I see it as an English Cotswold cottage. Lots of chintz and Jacobean furniture." She nudged a chair into a different position and picked up a green stone I had found on the road one day, turning it over as though it were a piece of china and the maker's mark might be on the underside. "Who takes care of the house for you?" she asked my father.

"Clair and I do it ourselves." He put his arm around me. "Cook, clean, and bottle-wash."

Uncle Keith quickly changed the subject. "Well, and how is the mission?"

Father described the schoolhouse. He was trying not to be too obvious about how pleased he was with the way things were going.

"You say the congregation is *up* to thirty?" My uncle and aunt exchanged glances.

"That's a considerable increase from June," Father pointed out.

"Well, they're very lucky to have someone with your abilities up here in the woods," Uncle Keith said.

Aunt Marcia smiled at me. "Clair, we've rented a cottage on the lake right outside of Blue Harbor. We want you to come and spend the weekend with us. We'll have you back on Monday."

"Wouldn't you like that, Clair?" my father asked. "I think it would be a pleasant change for you."

I wanted to say that I didn't need a change, that I would miss Dorrie. But the truth was, I was still a little giddy from the surprise of seeing my aunt and uncle and I couldn't get Westville Heights out of my mind. There

79

didn't seem to be any harm in a weekend with them. Besides, I wouldn't have to do any cooking or cleaning for a change and I would be back to see Dorrie on Monday.

"Well, you better get some clothes together." My Aunt Marcia could see I wanted to go with them.

"And have a shower," my father added. "And put on shoes. I'm afraid I've been a little lax in keeping up standards. Forget to dress for dinner in the jungle and all that."

My aunt and uncle gave him a funny look.

"I'm sure you do very well, David," Aunt Marcia said, and barely twitched as one of the five bureau-drawer mice, who now had the run of the house, flitted across the toe of her elegant sandal.

Aunt Marcia and Uncle Keith's "cottage" was about the size of a small hotel. Aunt Marcia said it had been built at the turn of the century as a summer home for a large family from Chicago who had made their money killing cows. The rooms were furnished with old wicker tables and chairs painted a fresh white. The thick green carpeting made you think the lawn had wandered into the house. On the walls were watercolors of brightly painted flowers in oranges and pinks and reds and yellows. When you stepped out the door into the garden there were the same flowers growing all around you. And from every window you looked through, the lake looked back at you.

Dinner was served on a large terrace by Emmy, the

lady who worked for my aunt and uncle. She knew me from Westville Heights and didn't even blink when I accepted seconds of lobster and chocolate souffle.

That night my aunt came to my room to help me unpack. As she shook my clothes out with a snap and laid them on the bed she said, "It doesn't look like you've worn these since you left Westville Heights, Clair. They're a bit wrinkled. I'll have Emmy touch them up with an iron." I could tell she was leading up to something else.

"Have you been happy up north, Clair?"

I shrugged. It seemed that the people who most liked to hear your confidences were exactly the ones you didn't want to confide in. Besides, I didn't like the way she and Uncle Keith had looked down their noses at our stone house.

"Your father told us you might come back to Westville Heights this winter. That's wonderful news. We've missed you so much. When I see you all I can think of is your poor mother." We both started getting teary. "But I don't want to bring back unhappy memories. Tomorrow we're going to take you into town. There're some super stores. I want to get you a present. A new dress or maybe something attractive for your bedroom. It looked a little — plain."

The next morning on the way into town, my Uncle Keith told me that years ago Blue Harbor had been a lumber port. When the trees had all been cut down, steamers began carrying vacationers north from Chicago. The little frame houses where the villagers had once lived were fashionable shops now with names like The Old Woman's Shoe and The Straw Stack.

Uncle Keith went off to play a set of tennis at the

Blue Harbor Club. "Leave a little something in the stores, you two," he called after us.

The first shop my aunt took me to sold old clothes and was called The Attic. Aunt Marcia tried to interest me in a gauzy white dress with ruffles and lots of lace. It must have been about a hundred years old. I couldn't think where I would ever wear it. I shook my head politely. She sighed and bought a real silk nightgown from the twenties. "It will make a perfect dress for the Peppers' cocktail party. I'm not likely to see someone else in the same thing." I thought Dorrie and I ought to take a good look at the clothes we found in the trash at the dump.

Next we went to a linen shop. "These pink-flowered sheets would be super in your room, Clair, and we could get the matching quilt for a bedspread. Just the thing for a country cottage."

But I shook my head again. I had hemmed a length of blue-checked cotton for a bedspread. My father had bought the material for me at the dollar store and sewing it had taken me a long time.

My aunt shrugged and bought a half-dozen green bath towels large as bed sheets and soft as moss.

When we met Uncle Keith at the club for lunch, Aunt Marcia shook her head. "Clair's hopeless, Keith. I don't know what we can do with her. She wouldn't let me buy her a thing."

"Well, there must be *something* you'd like, Clair," he said. He was wearing his tennis whites and looked quite handsome with his deep tan and his dark hair that had just a little white around the ears like my mice.

I nodded.

They looked so pleased I was embarrassed.

"Will you show us after lunch?"

I nodded again and they smiled at each other over my head, as though I not only couldn't talk, but couldn't see as well.

They weren't so happy when I led them to the hardware store, where I wandered around like someone in a dream. The shelves were filled with all the things Dorrie and I had longed for while we were building the sitting room. There were all kinds of nails and screws and hammers. There were even big sheets of plywood and stacks of lumber with practically no knotholes. My aunt and uncle were watching me. From the expression on their faces I thought I'd better make up my mind and pointed to some hinges. Dorrie would be able to put on her door.

"Hinges?" Uncle Keith said.

"Hinges?" Aunt Marcia repeated.

"Maybe they're for David's new church," Uncle Keith suggested.

"Yes, that must be it," my aunt said. She put her hand on my shoulder. "That's very thoughtful of you, Clair." I just smiled. I was thinking how excited Dorrie would be when she saw them. Uncle Keith gave me the package to carry. I loved the heaviness of it.

On the way home we passed a large sign that said HEMLOCK COUNTY SANITARY LANDFILL. I knew what that meant and grabbed at my Uncle Keith's arm so hard the car nearly swerved. I pointed at the sign, not caring what they thought.

Uncle Keith's voice was uncertain. "You want to go *there?* That's a dump!"

83

I looked as eager as I knew how.

"I don't believe I've been in the place. Our rubbish is picked up twice a week. However, I suppose it wouldn't hurt . . ." His voice trailed off and he looked doubtfully at Aunt Marcia.

She was looking straight ahead, her lips thinned into a tight line.

I imagined all the valuable things people in those large vacation houses might throw away and wondered how I could get my aunt and uncle to let me take them back with me for the sitting room. My mouth was dry with excitement.

The wide blacktop that led into the dump was a lot different from the rutted two-track trail into our own dump. But when we got to the landfill itself, I couldn't believe it. There was nothing to see but huge piles of sand. "Would you like to get out of the car and have a look?" my uncle asked, as though he were offering a view of some scenic spot.

As we got out of the car, a man walked over to us. "Can I help you folks? I'm afraid we're not open on Saturday afternoon."

"That's quite all right," my uncle said wryly. "We're just looking."

"Well, there's not much to see," the man said. "We bury the rubbish every night with our cat." He pointed to an enormous yellow bulldozer as big as a house. Its metal track shone from running through the sharp sand. "Covering everything over keeps the rats away and the odor down."

Suddenly I saw something that made me feel better. On the other side of our car was a large open space.

There were appliances, some of them like new, and lots of used furniture and piles of brightly colored magazines — not movie magazines, but the expensive kind like the ones Aunt Marcia kept on her coffee table.

The man saw me staring at all the loot. "That's salvage," he said. "A secondhand company comes and carries it away each Monday. We sell them exclusive rights. Anyhow" — he looked at my uncle's cashmere blazer and immaculate white slacks — "you wouldn't want that junk."

I walked slowly back to the car.

The next afternoon my aunt slipped onto the wicker sofa where I was reading a book. She put an arm around me, wafting the carnation smell in my direction. "Clair, dear, we've enjoyed having you this weekend. In fact, it's been so much fun, Uncle Keith and I wondered if you wouldn't like to spend the rest of the summer with us. Then you could join your father when the time comes to go back to Westville Heights. We're just the least bit worried about your being down there without any friends. Wouldn't you like to stay with us?"

I guess I panicked, because I shook my head and started to cry. The truth was that my weekend in Blue Harbor had been the loneliest one I had spent since I had left Westville Heights.

❧THIRTEEN

On Monday morning my aunt said she had a headache and Uncle Keith would drive me back. She looked sad when I left, sort of betrayed. The way you feel when a recipe you've carefully followed turns out to be a flop. She gave me a hug when I left, but I could tell her mind was on some more promising project.

On the way back Uncle Keith asked a lot of questions. Did I have friends? Did I get enough to eat? Was I happy? I kept nodding, and finally he stopped asking questions and began to whistle. I think my silence made him nervous. He thought when two people were together they ought to be talking. I could see he was relieved when we got to the stone house.

My father was outside watching for us. He looked upset. I wondered if Aunt Marcia had called him and complained about the way I had acted over the weekend. If she had, he didn't say anything. He was asking Uncle Keith about Blue Harbor when I slipped away to put the hinges in my room. As I started back into the living room I heard Uncle Keith say, "Really, Dave, I know you've had a hard time of it and maybe this little escape into the country is just the thing for you, but you have to think of Clair. To tell you the truth, Marcia and I noticed that she's really getting rather — different."

"How do you mean?" Father sounded worried.

"Well, she doesn't think much about her appearance and she seems to have lost all interest in the things girls her age are supposed to care about. I'll admit she looks healthy enough, but she still isn't talking. I mean that's strange."

"I'm afraid," my father said, "I've been too caught up in getting the church started. I haven't been keeping a close enough eye on Clair, but that's all going to change."

"I hope I haven't spoken out of turn."

"Not at all."

"Call on Marcia and me anytime. We're there if you need us."

I heard the screen door slam shut and the car drive away. Something in my father's voice had made me uneasy, but I had other things on my mind. I was anxious to change into my jeans and take the hinges over to Dorrie.

"Clair!" It was my father's pulpit voice. I started. He hadn't spoken to me like that since the devil's night I and some friends had toilet papered the headmaster's house with pink Charmin.

"Clair, I'm afraid I have something rather serious to say. After you left for Blue Harbor, I made some inquiries about Dorrie's grandmother and found out she wasn't staying at Dorrie's. When I paid her a visit she thought I was there for some sort of séance she was holding. She was rather inhospitable when she found out who I was. It took considerable persuasion and a lot of dodging of cats, but she finally admitted to me that Dorrie was living over at the pond all by herself.

"Of course I am unhappy that you would lie to me, Clair. However, it's not entirely your fault. I'm afraid I've been too preoccupied with getting the church underway. Your Uncle Keith was absolutely right to take me to task for not paying more attention to what you were up to. But you seemed to be taking hold so well. You were so happy. I even began to hope you might want to stay here this fall." My father's voice had gone from gruffly stern to sadly puzzled.

I spent a lot of time staring at my toes. My second toes are longer than my big toes. I used to think I was a freak, but my mother said it was a sign you had royal blood. I didn't know which was worse, my father's knowing that I had been lying to him or the possibility of Dorrie's having to go away.

He must have read my mind because he said, "I'm sure Dorrie is a resourceful child, but no thirteen-year-old should live by herself in the woods like that. I'm horrified when I think of the two of you alone there day after day. The Lord only knows what might have happened. The fact is, Clair, that Dorrie's father is being released from jail and it would be dangerous for her to be at their house when he gets out. He has an evil temper when he drinks and Dorrie just isn't safe with him.

"I talked with Mrs. Sepal from the child-welfare department. We decided it wouldn't be wise for Dorrie to go back to her grandmother's, so they've found a foster home for Dorrie. Dorrie is to go there this afternoon, but I persuaded Mrs. Sepal not to take her until you had a chance to say good-bye to Dorrie. They're waiting for us now."

I ran into my bedroom and grabbed the hinges, glad to have something to do, something to hold onto.

FOURTEEN

It was a still summer day. The pond had never looked so peaceful. Trees and grasses were mirrored in the water. The orange jewelweed hung over the bank looking at itself. How could they make Dorrie leave a place like the pond? I wished it had been an ugly day.

Dragging my feet, I followed my father toward the yard where Dorrie and Mrs. Sepal were waiting for us. Dorrie wouldn't look at me. "Hello, Reverend Lothrop," Mrs. Sepal said, "and this must be Clair."

Dorrie looked different. She wore shoes and a dress without holes. On the ground next to her was a small, sad-looking suitcase. "We're having a rather bad time of it today," Mrs. Sepal said.

What did she mean when she said *we're* having a bad time? It was Dorrie who was having the bad time.

My father looked at Dorrie and me, and then asked Mrs. Sepal if she wouldn't take a walk around the pond with him. "I think we should have a little chat," he said.

When they were out of hearing, Dorrie looked at me accusingly. "Your father turned me in."

I felt awful. All I could think of doing was to hand her the package with the hinges.

When she looked inside, she grinned as if she had forgiven me for having such an awful father. "They're *new!*" she said and quickly put them in her suitcase. "Percival's gone. Another woodchuck came and they went off into the woods. That's what I'd have done if I'd known who Mrs. Sepal was when she came. I could have run to the hideout and they never would have found me."

My father and Mrs. Sepal were back. Dorrie glared at them. "Maybe you can kidnap me and take me to some foster house, but the minute you leave, I'll run away. I'm not staying with any damn strangers."

"Dorrie," Mrs. Sepal said, "Reverend Lothrop and I have been talking. He has very kindly offered to let you come and live with Clair and himself."

Dorrie and I grabbed each other and started dancing around while Mrs. Sepal and my father tried to calm us down.

"I'll have to get my supervisor's approval for the plan," Mrs. Sepal warned.

"I'm afraid this will just be temporary," my father told us. "I mean our plans for the winter are uncertain."

We weren't listening. Dorrie had snatched up her suitcase and we were running for Guinevere. Dorrie untied her from the birch tree. "Come on," she called to my father, and we headed for the car.

"I hadn't . . . I'm afraid we can't . . . actually we don't have any place to keep a goat," my father finally got out. I thought he was a little stupid not to see that Dorrie couldn't just leave Guinevere.

"She'll stay in your yard," Dorrie assured him. "She'll keep the grass cut."

"But if it rains?"

"We can put her on your porch."

"The porch?"

"Yes, until I can make a lean-to in your backyard. I've got lumber left over from the sitting room. We can bring it over in the wheelbarrow."

"I believe the Rachetts have a goat. Couldn't we leave her with them?" my father suggested.

"They have a billy goat." Dorrie dismissed the idea. "Guinevere isn't used to men." She remembered my father. "Goatmen, that is."

Mrs. Sepal was laughing.

"Would your supervisor have to review any plan you made for the goat?" my father asked her. He was smiling, so I knew we had won.

"No," she said. "I'm sure she would feel Guinevere was in excellent hands."

"How will we get her home?" my father asked. "I suppose you two could walk her. Only I'm not too keen on letting either one of you out of my sight for a while."

"Oh, she can ride in the car," Dorrie told him. "She's very neat. She stays in the sitting room all the time."

My father's eyebrows nearly shot off his forehead. "There I put my foot down. No goats in the house!" But he let us lead Guinevere to our car and put her in the back seat where she nibbled on my father's hair all the way to the stone house.

❧ FIFTEEN

During her first days with us, Dorrie was nearly as silent as I was. She sat at the table staring hungrily at the food, not helping herself to anything until she saw how much we took. When my father said grace, Dorrie held herself stiffly upright, her hands folded on her lap, her eyes wide, as if something mysterious were taking place. I almost caught myself looking over my shoulder. Once she asked Father, "Could you pray that they keep my dad in jail?"

"Perhaps your father will have changed, Dorrie," he suggested. Dorrie was unconvinced and I was sure she had taken to praying on her own.

If my father really believed Mr. Norcher had turned into a nice person, he didn't show it. We weren't allowed to go back to the pond unless he went along. While we swam or read, he spent his time under the birch tree with Guinevere, working on his sermon. He even helped us put the door on the sitting room. Hang the door, he called it. He wouldn't go to the dump with us, though, even when we ran out of things to read. "Shopping bores me," was all he would say.

He took us to the library and got us each a card. I had always had one in Westville Heights, but it was the first one for Dorrie. She took out all the books they had on King Arthur — even the kind that had an index in the back and notes on the bottom of the page about stuff the author wasn't sure you wanted to know. "They don't tell you all the juicy stuff in the kids' books," she said. She was turning the pages a mile a minute.

When we weren't at the pond we were at the school-house. "I'll help you with your building projects," Father said, "if you help me with mine." It stayed light long enough into the summer evening so the men could come and work after their dinner. They had put a fresh coat of paint on the outside of the schoolhouse and polished the floors. Dorrie and I were given the job of raking and seeding the front yard, but I could see Dorrie longed to be in with the men learning how to use all their fancy power tools.

Mr. Simpson had made a cross out of western cedar. "Only thing'll hold up in these northern winters," he said. The minute the cross was nailed to the top of its peaked roof the school stopped being a school and looked like a church.

By the end of her first week with us Dorrie began to relax. She was excited about finally having an oven and baked acorn bread and Juneberry muffins. My father called it deer food. "I'm convinced we're all going to have fur and hooves by the time winter comes, Dorrie." But he was glad to see she felt at home.

Saturday evening my father was in his room putting the finishing touches on his sermon for the first service in the new church and Dorrie and I were out in front cutting clover for Guinevere when a car pulled up and Dorrie's grandmother got out. She passed right by us, hardly giving us a glance, and began pounding on the front door. My father came to the door and we started to follow her in but she slammed the screen door in our faces. "My business is with the Reverend," she said. "You two kids get lost!"

We lost ourselves under the open living-room window.

"What do you think you're doing grabbing that grandchild of mine right from under my nose?" we heard her say. "You've got no business mixing into our affairs. First the welfare stops my payments, and now I get a letter asking for restitution. Restitution! They want to rob me of what I got for taking care of that troublemaker."

"But Dorrie wasn't living with you. She was living by herself," Father pointed out.

"Was that my fault? Could I help it if she kept running away? I had all the worry of what could happen to her when she was at the pond by herself."

"Evidently you weren't worried enough to report it to the child-welfare worker."

"Norchers don't go turning one another in. We mind our own business. Not like some I could mention. What's Dorrie doing here anyway? She don't belong to you."

"The child-welfare office has given us permission to keep Dorrie here for a while."

"So *you* can get the payments."

"I've refused any payments. Dorrie is here as our guest."

"Well, I got news for you. My son was let out of jail today, and when he hears some strangers have got hold of his girl, he'll have a fit. Thorn Norcher isn't the kind to sit still for the government to run his family life.

"And I'll tell you something else. He's going to come stamping and snorting over to my house and want to know why Dorrie's not there, and what am I supposed to say? When he hears what happened he'll start slinging those cats around by their tails till the whole house'll be wallpapered with them.

"I'm taking that girl back with me right this minute. You just get her in here. I'm not having any dirty goat, though. You can sell the animal, if anyone will have it, and send the money to me."

Dorrie was ready to get Guinevere and head for the woods, but I signaled her to wait. I knew my father better than that.

"Mrs. Norcher!" Father's voice was hell and brimstone. "You aren't taking Dorrie anywhere! Dorrie has been placed here by the duly constituted authority of the court of Pine County. Take her away from here and you will be obstructing the law. For that, Mrs. Norcher, you could be sent to prison."

"Don't you threaten me just because I'm a helpless woman. I'm going to find my son, and when he hears you stole his child and tried to send his mother to jail, he'll take care of you good!"

We heard the screen door slam and the car start up. By the time we crawled out of our hiding place, she was gone. Dorrie looked worried. "My grandma'll tell my dad a pack of lies and he'll come after you," she said to Father. "I don't know if I ought to stay here. If I go away, maybe he'll leave you alone."

"Anyone who strikes women and children is a bully, Dorrie. He won't have the courage to come around here and challenge someone his own size. If he does, we have recourse to the law. You're not to worry. But I do want both of you to promise solemnly not to go wandering off on your own."

We promised. For the next couple of hours we sat on the front steps chewing sour grass and looking down the road, half afraid of what we might see. Nothing appeared but a porcupine. It waddled along slowly, its quills laid back, not noticing us until it was nearly in front of the house. Then it turned its back to us and raised its quills. When we didn't move, it put its quills back down and turned off into the woods, swinging its body from one side to the other. You had to laugh at how lukewarm it was about a fight. I hoped Dorrie's father would feel the same way.

Nothing else happened until two o'clock in the morning, when Father hurried into our rooms, woke us up, and told us to wrap ourselves in blankets and get outside quick. We ran stumbling through the dark house to the front yard, where my father was standing looking up at a sky curtained in yellows and greens and reds. It looked like someone had stretched a rainbow until it covered the whole sky. The rainbow faded and came again and faded and came again as though the sky were breathing the color in and out.

"Northern lights," Father said. "I suppose I shouldn't have wakened you, but it was too spectacular to miss." He didn't say why he had still been awake at that hour.

We put three chairs in the middle of the yard and sat wrapped up in our blankets, our heads tilted up. I hadn't even heard about northern lights. I wondered if there were other things like that I didn't know about.

We must have stayed out there over an hour. Dorrie and I didn't want to go in even when it began to get chilly and a cold, clammy ground fog started to rise around us, making our blankets damp. Father pointed to a line of stars. "Orion's belt," he said. "Fall is on its way." He sighed. I knew he was thinking about whether I would want to leave and go back to Westville Heights. I still thought I did. At the same time I wondered what would happen to Dorrie and how my father would feel about leaving the new church behind.

Lights came over the horizon that weren't northern lights. A car was driving toward us. When the driver picked the three of us up in his headlights he turned them off and slowed down. Father jumped up and told us to get into the house. We ran for the porch, but the car went right on past the house without stopping.

Before he sent us to bed Father made us each drink a cup of hot chocolate. But we stayed chilly all night.

🥀 SIXTEEN

We didn't really thaw out until breakfast the next morning when the sun came through the window, warming our backs and making stained glass out of the reflections on the table from our milk tumblers.

We were supposed to leave early, but Father was so rattled about holding his first service in the new church that it took him half an hour to find the notes for his sermon. When we finally got there, we could see several cars had already arrived. One of them had a flashing light. "Sheriff's car," Father said in a puzzled voice. "Wonder why he's here. Can't be so many people he has to direct traffic." A minute later we saw a fire engine and the black, smoldering shell of what had been the church. The smell of smoke was so strong it made your eyes water. The only thing that wasn't damaged was Mr. Simpson's cross.

Father stared and stared. Then he groaned and put his hands over his face. For a minute I was cross with the firemen because they were standing on the new grass Dorrie and I had planted and carefully marked off with a string fence tied with white cloth butterflies. Then I realized that now it didn't make any difference where they stood.

Dorrie said, "It was my dad."

"Surely not," my father told her. "No one would do a thing like that."

Dorrie shook her head. "It's just what he'd do," she said.

We climbed out of the car and walked slowly toward the others. Mr. Simpson met us. He didn't say a word, just put his hand on Father's shoulder. The others came up to us. They were all anxious to tell how they had felt when they drove up and saw what had happened. While we were listening to them the fire chief came over and apologized. "Sorry, Reverend. We got here quick as we could, but the fire just tore through the building." His face was shiny with sweat and there were sooty smudges on his nose and forehead. "I don't suppose you had insurance?" he asked. Father shook his head. When he wasn't the chief of the volunteer fire department, Mr. Dukey was the owner of the feed store where we bought grain for Guinevere. He'd let Dorrie and me watch the new chickens in the incubator, and sometimes he'd let us hold them in our hands.

Mr. Rachett asked, "Who'd be evil enough to do something like that, Reverend?"

Father quickly answered, "What makes you think someone did it? It might have been an accident."

"Oh, no," Mr. Dukey said. "Look what we found." He pointed to a kerosene tin.

"Last time we had any arson around here," Mr. Rachett said, "was when Thorn Norcher got drunk and tried to set fire to the bar in town."

Mrs. Rachett gave him a nudge and looked meaningly in the direction of Dorrie.

"We'll wait for more evidence before we come to any conclusions," Father said firmly, putting his arm around Dorrie's shoulders. But Dorrie moved out of the circle of his arm and stood by herself.

The sheriff came over and said something to Mr. Dukey. They turned to Father. "Mr. Rachett wasn't too far off base," Mr. Dukey said. "The sheriff just got a message on his radio from one of his deputies. Lady down the road said she saw Norcher this morning about seven o'clock. She was out feeding the chickens when he drove by. Sheriff's got a bulletin out for him."

Some of the congregation were starting to leave, but my father called them back. "It's Sunday morning," he said, "and we'll have our service as usual." People sort of looked at one another and then arranged themselves self-consciously in front of where my father was standing. Everyone was perfectly quiet, even the Rachetts' kids. After the reading from the gospel, Father said, "I hope you don't mind if I depart a bit from my prepared sermon." He looked around at everyone. "We have put together two structures, my friends. The one built of wood and nails has been destroyed. The other still stands, stronger than ever. That second structure is the friendship and sense of community that has been built among us during the long hours we worked together. It is the *first* structure that *we* beheld. But it was the second structure that God watched grow. That second structure can never be destroyed."

101

When it came time for the collection, Mr. Simpson borrowed a hard hat from one of the firemen and passed it around. People dug into their pockets and when the hat went past me I could see ten- and twenty-dollar bills. We'd never had more than a five before, and that had been only once and plenty special.

When the service was over, Mr. Simpson came up to Father and said they'd all be there Monday after dinner to start cleaning things up and see what could be salvaged.

While they were talking, I looked around for Dorrie. When I couldn't see her, I went to the car, expecting her to be waiting for us, but the car was empty. A page from the sermon Father had never had a chance to use was lying on the steering wheel with a note penciled on the back of it.

Dear Rev. Lothrop,

I am too much trouble because of my dad so I'm going away. I'm sorry about the church. If I can get a job, I'll send you some money. Clair can have Guinevere.

Yours truly,
Doreen Norcher

🌺 SEVENTEEN

The sheriff helped us look for Dorrie. My father had wanted me to stay with the Simpsons while he and the sheriff went hunting for her, but I got in the sheriff's car with him, leaving the Simpsons standing on the sidewalk.

Dorrie wasn't at the pond or at her grandmother's. No one in town had seen her. There were no reports from the state police of a hitchhiker who met Dorrie's description. "I should never have let her out of my sight," Father said. "I was thinking more about the loss of the church than about how Dorrie might feel. *Things* again instead of *people*. I'm afraid I'll never learn."

We spent the afternoon driving up and down the country roads. Ordinarily I would have been excited about cruising around with a sheriff and listening in on all the frightening radio messages that were delivered in a relaxed, chatty voice. But all I could think about was Dorrie. I had this picture in my mind of her running and her father right behind her and getting closer. What I didn't know was that when that happened I was going to be there, too.

The sheriff drove with one hand on the wheel and the other hand stuck out of his window resting on the top of the car roof. While he was carrying on a conversation with Father and the radio at the same time, he was looking along the road and behind the bushes and trees, not missing a thing. Once he slammed on the brakes and was out of his car and into the brush, where he dragged out two boys who met a description we had heard minutes before on the radio. The boys had been seen near a car where a tape deck had been reported stolen. They still had it on them and the sheriff handcuffed them and shoved them into the back of the car. He looked so serious you would have thought he was taking in two murderers. But when he came back from the county jail where he had delivered them he was smiling. "The handcuffs and ride to the jail will just about take care of those kids — that and what their folks'll do to them."

It was supper time when he dropped us off at the stone house. There hadn't been a trace of Dorrie. I'm not sure what we had for supper. I think it was tuna-fish sandwiches. It seemed like any time there was a crisis and we couldn't pull ourselves together enough to cook a meal, we opened a can of tuna fish. Even the smell of tuna made me feel like disaster was on the way.

After dinner I went out in the front yard and sat next to Guinevere. She was munching hay. The stems disappeared into her mouth like strands of spaghetti. I kept looking down the road, but it stayed empty. It was about then that I remembered Dorrie's hideout. I was sure she had spent the day there.

What I should have done was to tell my father. But I remembered how the sheriff had taken the two boys to jail — even if it had been only to scare them. What if you were breaking the law when you ran away? If you were, I would be turning Dorrie in.

Trying to look tired, I went into my bedroom with a glass of milk and a peanut-butter sandwich. I had a book under my arm. My father didn't seem suspicious. All he said was, "Get a good night's sleep, dear. We'll try again tomorrow. And don't worry. If anyone can look after herself, it's Dorrie." But he didn't sound convinced.

I waited a few minutes and then climbed out of my window. Now that it was late August, night came earlier. As I walked along Three Mile Road the wild asters and the night-blooming primroses were only dim spots of color. That afternoon while we were riding around we had seen an oak tree darken as hundreds of flocking blackbirds on their way south had settled on its branches. I had been anxious for fall to come because it meant before long I would be in Westville Heights. But now, looking back on the summer with Dorrie, my summers in Westville Heights seemed dull. I hardly knew the Clair Lothrop who had lived there.

I started into the woods, nervous at the way darkness had changed the familiar path to a strange landscape of dim shapes and queer noises. I realized I was stupid to come by myself, but somehow I felt it was too late to turn back. By the time I got to Dorrie's it was dark. In the moonlight the pond was a silver circle, and walking across the yard I walked over the long black moon-shadows of the trees.

Someone whispered my name and Dorrie ran out of the woods. The next minute we were climbing up into the sitting room. "I heard someone coming down the road," Dorrie said. "I was afraid it was my father. Boy, was I relieved when it turned out to be you. I was going to run away this morning but I didn't have any clothes or money or anything, so I had to come back here. I stayed in the hideout until it got dark. Before I go, you've got to help me have a séance. I can't have one by myself. I want to materialize my ma and maybe she'll tell me what to do."

I had never wanted to talk so much in my life. I wanted to tell Dorrie that what she should do was to come back to our house. But no words would come out. Dorrie closed the curtains and draped a towel over the mirror. "My grandma always put something over the windows and mirrors," she said, "so the spooks don't see themselves.

"We have to hold hands and concentrate." Dorrie lit a candle and placed it in the middle of the table. She sat down and motioned me to sit across from her. I tried to show Dorrie I didn't want to have any part of a séance. I didn't believe you could bring things back from the dead like that. And even if you could, how did you know *what* you might bring back? But Dorrie insisted. "Come on," she said. In the candlelight Dorrie's face was a mask of jerking shadows. I was half afraid of her. "Come on," she said impatiently.

I sat down at the table and took Dorrie's outstretched hands. They felt cold. "You have to keep quiet and wait,"

106

Dorrie said. "We should hear something give a knock or feel the table bounce around. The time I watched at my grandma's we heard this funny voice. It sounded like an old record, but it might have been someone who was dead a long time. Keep concentrating." Dorrie closed her eyes.

I tried to close mine, but they wouldn't stay shut. I blinked and thought I saw something move. My eyes flew open. The door had swung wide and a shadow was moving along the wall of the room. I clutched Dorrie's hands.

"What the hell is going on here!" It was a man I had never seen before, but I knew from the look on Dorrie's face that it was her father. The sloped ceiling kept him hunched over, and his shadow against the wall looked like a crouching animal.

Dorrie and I were holding hands harder than ever. We didn't seem to be able to let go. He stared at us and then at the draped mirror. "You having some kind of hocus-pocus like that fake stuff my ma does? You know what she used to do when I was a kid? Make me sit in the basement and poke a broomstick through a hole in the floor to make the table move." He sat down. "I'll just join your little party. I brought my own refreshments." He was smiling, but it didn't suit his face. "Get me a glass, Dorrie. It's not polite to drink out of a bottle." Dorrie let go of my hand and got him a jelly glass. He poured some liquor into the glass and drank it right down like they do in the westerns.

"I got a dime for sittin' down in that filthy basement and moving the table. And I got a dime for knocking on the living-room ceiling. I got a dime for playing the phonograph. And after it was all over, I got a whipping because I never done it just right. But I had my thirty cents."

He turned to me. "I suppose you're the minister's brat. You tell your dad I don't like him butting into my affairs. He's got no business taking my daughter away from me. I guess I showed him that this morning." He laughed and poured another drink. He didn't drink it, though, he just sat looking at it. "I'm taking you with me, Dorrie. I'm hitching a ride downstate and then over to Canada. Much better chance hitchin' with a kid. People trust you." He emptied the glass.

"I'm not going anywhere with you," Dorrie told him.

He reached across the table and slapped her face. "Where'd you learn that sass? That what you learned from the Reverend?" He turned to me. "We'll just fix it so you can't get away from here till Dorrie and me are too far for anyone to follow after us."

I had never seen an adult hit someone. Suddenly I understood that there had always been rules in my life and that because things like that were against those rules they had never happened to me. But outside of my life, in the lives of some other people, there were no rules and anything could happen. Then I realized that now I was a part of those other lives and that anything might happen to me, too.

"What'd you do to this place, Dorrie? What'd you build this crummy shack on top of my house for? People see this, they think I'm nuts and laugh at me."

"It's a sitting room," Dorrie said. Her voice was just a whisper.

"It's coming down. I'm not having nothing like this on top of my house." He kicked at one of the walls until it shattered, leaving a gaping hole.

"You stop it!" Dorrie shouted.

He just laughed and started kicking at another wall. The mirror fell to the floor and shattered. Dorrie ran at him and began pounding at him with her fists. He stood there laughing at her. Then he stopped laughing and grabbed her by the shoulder and spun her around, throwing her against the table. "You're a devil just like your ma was, but you ain't getting away with it anymore than she did. I'll teach you a lesson you won't forget."

He was standing across the table from Dorrie and me. As he started for Dorrie, she pushed the table over, knocking him off balance, sending the candle crashing to the floor and leaving the room in darkness. Her father gave a howl of rage. I felt Dorrie grab my hand and pull me toward the door. Her father heard us. "Oh, no, you don't." He struck a match and for a moment we were trapped in its light. He started for us, but the match went out. He lit another, but by then we were out the door and scrambling across the yard.

Dorrie headed straight for the pond. I thought she didn't know where she was going and tried to pull her toward the woods. But she dragged me onto the raft and, wading into the water, pushed it off. "Untie the rope, quick," she said, "or he'll pull us back to shore." She was holding onto the edge of the raft and kicking her feet to push it toward the middle of the pond. I tried to untie the knot but the rope was wet and hard to loosen. We felt a tug as the raft was yanked back toward the shore.

"Wait till I get a hold of you two!" Dorrie's father shouted, his voice echoing over the pond. We were almost at the shore, when the knot gave way and the raft was free. We heard him splash toward us and saw him standing in the moonlight a few feet away. Dorrie was kicking hard. "We're O.K. now," she said. "It's over his head out here and he can't swim."

We kept the raft hovering in the middle of the pond by taking turns slipping into the water and kicking. Once we heard Mr. Norcher call out, "You'll get tired and then it'll be my turn!" In the white light of the moon we could see him sitting on the shore, his back propped up against the birch tree where we used to tie Guinevere. "He'll sit there and drink all night," Dorrie whispered.

A breeze had started up, and we had to kick hard to keep the raft from drifting out of the deep water. The breeze was blowing little clouds across the moon. When the sky darkened everything became invisible and we had no way of knowing how close to shore we were drifting or where Mr. Norcher was.

It seemed like hours went by. Each time we climbed out of the water onto the raft, we started to shiver. Our legs were tired from kicking and our hands were so cramped we could hardly hold onto the raft. We began taking shorter and shorter turns. Once Dorrie fell asleep on the raft and I had to shake her to get her to wake up and take her turn.

I felt my eyes begin to close. Great weights were pressing down on my eyelids. I thought I would close them for just a second. When I started awake, the raft was drifting and I couldn't hear the sound of Dorrie's kicking. I thought she must have climbed on the raft and was waiting for me to get into the water and take my turn. The moon was behind the clouds, and I couldn't see anything. I felt along the deck of the raft, but Dorrie wasn't there. She had to be in the water.

If I jumped in and started to swim around looking for her, the raft would drift away from both of us. But if I didn't jump in Dorrie would drown or maybe she already had. I slipped into the water and prayed that I could find her.

"Dorrie!" I called, "Dorrie!"

I had spoken after all those silent months! I still had a voice! Nothing that evening frightened me more than hearing myself call out. I didn't know where my voice had come from, only that it was finally back. "Dorrie!"

"Over here." It was only a faint sound. I swam in the direction I thought it had come from, pulling myself along with my arms. My legs were so tired from kicking I could hardly move them. I heard Dorrie struggling to stay above the water. With two more strokes I reached her and held on. A cloud pulled away from the moon. We could see the raft drifting toward the shore where Dorrie's father was waiting. He was slumped over. I pulled Dorrie toward the opposite shore. If we could reach it before her father saw us, we might be able to get to the hideout. I was sure I couldn't swim another inch, when I felt the soft muck of the pond bottom under my feet. Dorrie felt it at the same moment and we began to run through the water. The pond lilies and rushes brushed our legs. Then we were on the shore.

We heard a shout come from across the pond. Dorrie's father had seen the empty raft. He began running heavy-footed toward us. The moon lit up the tops of the trees, but under the canopy of leaves everything was dark, too dark to follow the path to the brook. We scrambled over brush piles and tree stumps, trying to keep from crying out when we stumbled. The low branches tore at our hair and slapped against our faces. We could hear Dorrie's father behind us, tracking us by the sounds we made. My side ached and the bottoms of my feet were raw. Our wet clothes clung to us like an icy hand. There was a moment when the footsteps seemed right behind us. Twice there was the sound of a fall and cursing and someone pulling himself up.

Then we felt a trickle of cold water under our feet. The next minute we were running along the brook toward the hideout. We heard Mr. Norcher splashing along behind us, but the sky had darkened again and the footsteps seemed farther off. Dorrie pulled me down and we crawled under the shelter of the woven branches. The footsteps came closer — were right beside the hideout — passed us.

We wrapped ourselves in the blankets and waited. It seemed like hours went by with no sound but the distant hooting of an owl. It would have been comforting to talk, but we were afraid to say a word. Mr. Norcher could have crept back and might be close by, waiting for us to give ourselves away. Sometime toward morning we fell asleep.

EIGHTEEN

I was awakened by Dorrie's coughing and I opened my eyes to see the sun shining through the branches of the hideout roof. My back was sore from sleeping on the ground and my hands had blisters on them from hanging onto the raft. Apart from that I was surprised to find I was all right.

But Dorrie wasn't. "I feel like somebody poured boiling water down my throat," she said. Her voice was raspy.

"Shouldn't we try to get out of here right away?" I asked her, relieved to find my voice was still there.

Dorrie didn't seem surprised to hear me speak.

"We can't go to the pond. My dad might still be there. If we tried to get out through the woods, we'd get lost. Then he'd find us for sure. He knows all the trails from trapping. I think we should stay here till it's dark again. When I feel a little better I'll get us something to eat from the berry bowl." Her face was red, her eyes watery. She slumped down into her blanket, and I could tell she had fallen asleep again.

I was too worried to go back to sleep, so I sat listening to the wind moving the branches of the trees over our heads. If I were in Westville Heights now, I thought, I'd probably be on the phone with someone trying to think of something to do. At the start of summer vacation you were sure you'd never run out of stuff. By August you were down to things like writing anonymous love letters to the lifeguard at the club and going to makeup demonstrations for teens at the local department store. I wondered what my friends would think if they could see me sitting in the middle of the woods waiting for something awful to happen.

Finally I got up enough courage to crawl outside. The sun shining through the morning mist made the whole forest look like an invisible fire was filling it with smoke. Chickadees were flying from tree to tree calling to one another. A little farther off an olive-backed bird with an orange spot on its head saw me and took off. I thought the birds were probably a good sign. They wouldn't have been there if someone were nearby. I drank some of the dark water from the creek and ate a handful of blooming watercress, white flowers and all. It made my mouth feel fresh and I wondered why someone didn't invent watercress toothpaste. That was the kind of dumb thing I thought about to keep from thinking of how, with Dorrie sick, it would be up to me to find something for us to eat.

In the distance I could see where the trees seemed to thin out and decided that must be the berry bowl. I started toward it, stopping every few minutes to listen for sounds. Once I passed an enormous pine tree and rubbed its needles between my fingers for the comfort of their piney fragrance.

As I walked toward it, the opening in the woods seemed to move away. It was taking me such a long time to reach it I wondered if I had been wrong to leave Dorrie. I was about to turn back when I stepped through a thick screen of hemlock and found myself in an open field shaped like a bowl. It was yellow with goldenrod and covered with blackberry bushes. At first all I saw were the berries that had been dried into thimbles of seed by the sun. But hidden under the leaves were purple berries as big as my thumb. I stuffed a handful into my mouth and felt the juice run down my chin. They tasted the way perfume smells, but the seeds were real enough.

I began to fill an old tin can I had found with berries for Dorrie. I had nearly finished when a particularly ripe and juicy berry slipped out of my fingers and onto the ground. As I reached down for it, I saw a hole only inches from where I was standing. Some animal, I thought, lucky enough to have a berry patch in his own backyard. Then a gleam of metal caught my eye and I saw one of Mr. Norcher's set traps fastened to a stake. The cruel steel teeth were propped open waiting for a victim. It might have been me. I backed away carefully from the trap. My first impulse was to run to the hideout as quickly as I could. But what if there were other traps set around the bowl? I forced myself to walk slowly, searching every inch as I went along until I was safely out of the bowl.

All that time under the hot sun made me a little dizzy. When I closed my eyes everything was red and I could feel my heart pounding. My hair and clothes were clammy with sweat. When I finally reached the woods I wanted to sink down in the cool shade and rest, but I made myself keep going by counting my steps and telling myself when I got to five hundred I'd be back at the hideout. But I wasn't. I counted to a thousand and then two thousand and still I wasn't there. Nothing looked familiar. Dorrie had once explained to me how you could tell the direction you were traveling by the sun. Why hadn't I paid more attention?

I must have walked for nearly an hour when I saw an opening in the trees and realized I was back at the berry bowl. I had traveled in a circle. Across the bowl I could see the screen of hemlocks I had first walked through. I felt as though someone had played a trick on me and switched everything around. What had happened was that I had been so occupied looking down at the ground for traps, I had entered the woods from the wrong side. I dragged myself across the bowl, the heat from the sun nearly melting me. When I wet my dry lips with my tongue I could taste salt from the sweat running down my face. Finally I was back in the woods. I passed the large pine and in a few more minutes I was at the hideout.

It was hot and stuffy inside, but Dorrie had both blankets wrapped around her and her teeth were chattering. "I was hot a minute ago," she said in a hoarse voice, "now I'm freezing. Where were you?"

I handed her the berries and told her about the trap. She only ate about two of the berries. I tried to remember what my mother used to say about feeding a cold and starving a fever. Or was it the other way around? "As soon as it's dark I can see if there's anyone at the pond," I told her. After getting lost such a short distance from the hideout I dreaded another walk through the woods, but I could see Dorrie needed a doctor.

"How come you started talking last night?" Dorrie asked in a weak whisper.

"I guess I just wanted to." I didn't mention how Dorrie had nearly drowned.

"You mean you could have talked all along if you had wanted to?"

"I honestly don't know. I think it had a lot to do with wanting to go back to Westville Heights."

"And you don't want to now?"

I shook my head, then remembered I didn't have to do that anymore. "No," I said. I think I had known ever since I had come back from Blue Harbor that I would never go back to Westville Heights to live. I told Dorrie about the Blue Harbor sanitary landfill.

"I don't think that's very democratic," she said. "Everybody ought to have a right to their neighbor's trash."

She fell asleep for a while, and when she woke she seemed a little better and ate some more blackberries. We even started to make plans for rebuilding the sitting room. "Do you think your father would let us use his saw," she asked, "or is he mad at me because of what my father did to his church?"

"He's not mad at you, he's mad at your father. Anyhow, they're going to rebuild the church. I'm going to tell him to use our station-wagon money. We don't need it now if we're not going back." I explained to Dorrie about the station wagon. "Maybe," I told her, "we could save out enough to buy some trout fingerlings for the pond." I thought that might make her feel better, but when I looked she was asleep.

Each time she took a breath I could hear wheezing noises like air coming out of a balloon. I was hungry, but I didn't dare leave her again. While she slept I sat just outside the hideout without anything to do but think. Each thought was worse than the one before. I thought of Dorrie getting sicker and of my losing my way in the woods and of Mr. Norcher looking for us and hearing Dorrie cough. I wondered why you didn't have pleasant thoughts when you were by yourself and could pick out any you wanted to.

Late in the afternoon we heard something moving through the woods. At first we thought it might be a deer, but as it came closer to us we could make out the crunch of boots walking heavily over the ground. My first impulse was to run out of the hideout and let whoever it was know we were there. But the look of fear on Dorrie's face told me to stay right where I was. While we waited silently for the boots to move past us, Dorrie kept her hands over her mouth and struggled to keep from coughing. When the sound of the boots had disappeared, Dorrie looked relieved, but I wasn't so sure. Instead of Mr. Norcher, it might have been our one chance for help.

NINETEEN

When it was nearly dark I woke Dorrie, who had fallen into a fidgety sleep, and told her I was leaving. She wanted to go with me, but when she tried to stand up she was light-headed and her coughing started again. "If your father's there he'd hear you a mile away," I told her and made her lie back down.

"Don't let him catch you," she said. "After last night I don't know what he'd do." At that I nearly turned back.

It was still light enough so that I could follow the brook. At the edge of the woods I hid behind the trees, waiting for the dark when I could creep out to see if there were any signs of Mr. Norcher. If there weren't, I'd head for the stone house. If Mr. Norcher were still at the pond, I would have to go back to the hideout and try again the next night. And by that time I didn't know how sick Dorrie would be.

If you're not looking at it the sky gets dark quickly

like a shade pulled down, but if you're just sitting and waiting for it to happen, the change from day to night takes forever. When darkness finally did come, I was afraid to move, and it was several minutes before I could bring myself to begin inching toward the pond.

The Norchers' house was nothing more than a shadow and the pond a dark field. I moved a little way out into the yard. The next second the yellow eye of a flashlight beam swept across my face. I felt as though its beam had scorched me. The light clicked off and I heard footsteps running in my direction. I dove for the cover of the woods, the footsteps right behind me. I had only taken a few steps when the sound of a car stopped me. It stopped Mr. Norcher, too.

We both kept perfectly still, watching the car come to a halt. Two men got out and began cautiously circling the yard. If Mr. Norcher hadn't been so close to me, I could have called out, but I was sure he would get to me before they could. Suppose he took me hostage or something. I just stood there, paralyzed.

One of the men went through the cellar and the sitting room while the other one crisscrossed the yard. Then they both got into their car and drove away. I stood there waiting for Mr. Norcher to make the first move. But he was waiting for me. Minutes went by and then he must have become impatient, because he started flailing around the woods looking for me. Each time he moved, I moved. When he was still, I was still. I didn't dare lead him too close to the hideout for fear he'd hear Dorrie coughing. But if I went too far away from it I'd lose myself in the woods and never get back to her.

I stumbled through a thick hedge of trees and found

myself in the berry bowl. With no cover to hide my movements it was the worst possible place to be, but with Mr. Norcher right behind me I couldn't turn around. I was concentrating on finding a way to double back before he could make a grab for me, when I heard metal snap and then a howl followed by thrashing noises and furious swearing. Mr. Norcher's footsteps had stopped.

I remembered the trap with its open mouth of steel teeth. He would have to pry the teeth apart. That would take time. I ran for the hideout, Mr. Norcher's curses growing fainter as I ran. I passed a giant shadow and knew it was the pine tree. A minute later I stepped into the glare of a searchlight and heard my father call my name. We ran toward each other and sort of collided. I was laughing and crying and trying to tell him everything that had happened.

The first thing he said to me was, "You're talking!"

I thought that was pretty obvious. "Where's Dorrie?" I asked. "Is she all right?"

"She will be as soon as we get her someplace warm and find a doctor for her."

"Mr. Norcher's caught in one of his traps. He's in the berry bowl."

The sheriff was standing next to us. "Where's that?" He motioned over some men. I recognized Mr. Simpson and Mr. Rachett. Mr. Simpson said, "I've hunted there. I can show you."

"How did you find us?" I asked Father. I had his hand and was pulling him toward the hideout.

"We knew you must be in the woods. Two of the sheriff's deputies saw your footprints near the pond this evening. They saw Mr. Norcher's, too," he added and held on hard to my hand. "We thought you were in the woods, but we had searched there all day and hadn't discovered any trace of you."

"We heard someone come right by us," I said, "but we were afraid it was Dorrie's father, so we just stayed in the hideout and kept quiet."

"Well, your hideout was extremely effective. All the men from the congregation and the sheriff and his deputies couldn't discover it. But this evening I had an inspiration."

I waited for him to tell me, but he just smiled and said, "Come and see."

Dorrie was standing outside the hideout, draped all over with blankets and drinking something from a thermos. She had a wide grin on her face and one arm around Guinevere, who was nibbling contentedly on the edge of a blanket.

My father said, "I remembered your telling me that Guinevere used to go for walks in the woods with you, so we brought her out here and she led us to the hideout. Well, not exactly *right* to it . . ."

". . . I heard her bleating and ran out," Dorrie put in, finishing his sentence. "Clair, I told your father you don't want to go back to Westville Heights."

My father turned to me. "Is that true, Clair?" He looked doubtful, as though he had heard some news that was too good to be true.

"Yes," I said, and told him I wanted the station-wagon money used to rebuild the church.

"Only if you and Dorrie promise to give us a hand with the construction."

"We'll have to build that lean-to for Guinevere first;

122

the winter's coming." Dorrie paused. "There's just one thing. If the snow gets too deep and we can't get out twice a day to milk her we might have to keep Guinevere in the house."

My father sighed. "Certainly. After tonight I'd be pleased to turn my bedroom over to her if necessary. Perhaps we could get your Aunt Marcia to decorate it for Guinevere."

One of the deputies carried Dorrie to our car and settled her in the front seat. I climbed in next to her and Guinevere got in the back. My father turned up the collar of his shirt. "We've called Doc Mason," the deputy said. "He's already on his way to your place."

As we started out for the stone house the sheriff's car went flying past us, the lights flashing and the siren shrieking. I got a glimpse of Mr. Norcher in the back seat. Dorrie didn't look. Dad told us arson was a serious charge. Her father would be in jail for a long time, but she didn't seem as pleased as I expected. I didn't know why.

Dr. Mason was waiting for us on our porch. "Well, Reverend," he said, "so you've been romping around the woods in the middle of the night. You city folk have some funny ways of amusing yourselves. Next time you take a notion to play hide-and-go-seek, I'd be obliged if you'd do it in the daytime." Then he got a good look at Dorrie and didn't say anything more. He just went to work with his stethoscope.

I was afraid he would take Dorrie to the hospital, but he left us some pills and said, "These little fellows ought to do the trick. I'll be back first thing in the morning. Have the coffeepot on for me. And for heaven's

123

sake stay in the house tonight, will you? I'd like to get some sleep."

Dorrie went right to bed, but I was wide awake.

"It's the excitement," my father said. "How about a peanut-butter sandwich? You must be starved."

"Why wasn't Dorrie happy that her father was going to jail? I thought that's what she wanted." I had been thinking about the way Dorrie wouldn't look at her father in the sheriff's car.

"There must have been times these last months, Clair, when you came close to hating me for taking you away from Westville Heights."

I didn't say anything.

"Well, there must be times when, in spite of everything, Dorrie comes close to loving her father."

That made me feel awful, and I had a second peanut-butter sandwich. I had just gotten to the center part where the most butter and peanut butter always were, when my father asked, "Clair, what made you decide you didn't want to go back to Westville Heights?"

"It's so boring there," I told him.

"You don't suppose we'll always have this kind of excitement here, do you?"

I didn't see why not.

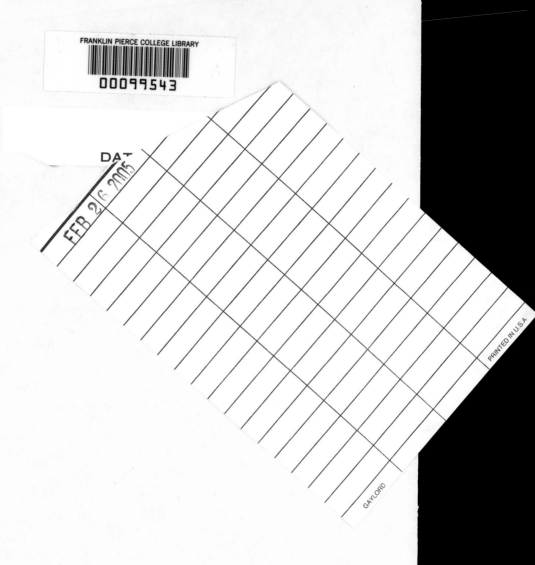